NEW FRIENDS
IN NEW PLACES

Books in the Forever Friends series

New Friends in New Places (Book One)
Friends Make the Difference (Book Two)
Summer of Choices (Book Three)
Collinsville High (Book Four)

New Friends in New Places

Lynn Craig

THOMAS NELSON PUBLISHERS
Nashville • Atlanta • London • Vancouver

Published in Nashville, Tennessee, by Thomas Nelson, Inc.,
Publishers, and distributed in Canada by Word
Communications, Ltd., Richmond, British Columbia.

Library of Congress Cataloging-in-Publication Data

Craig, Lynn.
   New friends in new places / Lynn Craig.
      p.   cm. — (Forever friends series : bk. 1)
     Summary: Fourteen-year-old Katelyn begins a journal
writing about her adjustment to high school in a new
town and her idea to start a Christian friends club.
    ISBN 0-8407-9239-5 (pbk.)
    [1. Moving, Household—Fiction. 2. High schools—
Fiction. 3. Schools—Fiction. 4. Friendship—Fiction.
5. Diaries—Fiction. 6. Clubs—Fiction. 7. Christian
life—Fiction.] I. Title. II. Series: Craig, Lynn. Forever
friends series : bk. 1.
PZ7.C84426Ne 1994
[Fic]—dc20   93–1929
                                                 CIP
                                               AC

Printed in the United States of America.
1 2 3 4 5 6 — 99 98 97 96 95 94

To

my darling goddaughters
Katelyn and Kiersten

Chapter One

Unwelcome Words

Thursday
8 P.M.

"I hear you're going to McKinney."

I am one hundred percent, positively-without-question convinced that I have never heard six more devastating words in all my life. Well, at least in the last month or two.

And that, dear Journal, is why I am writing in you. There's really nobody else in whom I can confide this awful turn of events. Normally I would be able to tell all this—at least most of it—to my Aunt Beverly, but she's away on a buying trip, so I have done the next best thing. I have purchased you, dear Journal—well, actually, not yet, but I will as soon as Aunt Beverly gets back—from her wonderful book, stationery, and gift store at 4th and Elm. In the end, you will probably be a

1

gift to me, but either way, I will cherish you always. I promise.

I should perhaps also tell you that I have decided to formally call you my "Journal." I read somewhere that writers for eons and decades have kept journals, and since I aspire to be a writer someday, I am choosing to follow in their tradition. That probably means, of course, that I will be telling you far more than the normal diary writer. I'm into dialog and incredibly long and involved descriptions—at least that's what my family has told me for years. My entries will probably be longer than usual, since my family tells me that I also tend to ramble. All of which means that you will probably be joined someday by other journals on my secret shelf. Well, so be it. For now, it's just you and me. And considering that I have made no other friends here in Collinsville, I have lots to tell you.

Where to begin? That's really the question of questions for the moment.

Perhaps I should tell you a little about myself, so you'll better understand why those six words—spoken to me in a quite startling and abrupt manner during the noon break today—have left me crushed, absolutely crushed.

My name is Katelyn Anna Louise Weber. Anna and Louise were the first names of my grandmothers, and Katelyn was the name of my mother's best friend as a little girl. I like having names that relate to other people. It's fun to imagine in what ways we might be alike.

I am fourteen and a half and fairly tall for my age, but in all other ways, I am boringly average. At least I think so. Grandpa tells me I'm pretty, and so does Aunt Beverly after she's fixed my hair, but mostly I feel average. My eyes are green, my hair a rather dark blond in the summer and a light brown in the winter. It's somewhat longish—about to my shoulders, I guess—and wavy, which is very troublesome. I'd rather it be curly or straight. My hair is the one thing in my life that is the most unlike me. I can nearly always make up my mind about things very quickly and very decisively— my hair, on the other hand, is entirely unpredictable! It seems to have a mind of its own, and I'm never quite sure what it's going to agree to do. I'm supposed to wear glasses when I read, and since I seem to be reading most of the time, I wear glasses most of the time. Aunt Beverly tells me that I have a "darling figure," but I'm not sure entirely what that means. I think of "darling" as being a word that goes with petite girls, and as I said, I'm pretty tall.

In personality, I know I'm a bit stubborn— sometimes a lot stubborn—and I'm also a little shy. I'd rather watch people for a while before I decide to get to know them. I love to read and to write stories, and as I said, I want to be a writer someday. I'll probably also be a teacher, or perhaps I'll have a shop like Aunt Beverly's, since I've heard that it's difficult to get published when you are just starting out as a writer. I'm willing to keep trying though, as long as it takes. Someday I'll be a novelist. It's just something I know about myself. And that's another thing about me—I know myself pretty well. I'm honest about my faults, but mostly I like who I am. I like to play softball and tennis, but I'm terrible at basketball and I wish somebody would teach me the rules of football. I like to watch the game, but I don't always understand what's going on. I like buttermilk more than soft drinks, which most people think is really weird. That doesn't bother me—at least not enough for me to give up drinking buttermilk. I know how to knit and play the piano. Gramma Weber taught me to knit and Mom taught me to play the piano. Once I make a friend, I'm very loyal. I love my family and I like to try new things.

So much for me. I should probably tell you a little about my family, too. I have a younger sister named Kiersten. She's ten, and we really get along pretty well, except for the times when she's on what I call a "question kick." Sometimes she asks a million questions about everything, which can be very frustrating when she doesn't wait for the answer to one question before asking another one!

4

Kiersten has red hair and green eyes. She gets the red hair from Dad, whose name is Oliver Fred Weber. He goes by Fred—but, of course, he's Dad to us. Dad works in the hardware store with Grandpa Stone, who is my mother's father—which means, I guess, that Dad and Grandpa are "in-laws." It doesn't feel that way, though. Grandpa treats Dad like a son as best I can tell. Stone's Hardware has been in our family for generations. Grandpa told me once that my great-great grand-father—Edgar Stone—was a blacksmith and he started the shop as part of his service to the ranchers and farmers who came to him from miles around.

Aunt Beverly, whom I've already mentioned several times, is Dad's sister. I'm like my Aunt Beverly in lots of ways, although I don't look a great deal like her. Aunt Beverly is about my height, but her hair is a lot darker and naturally curly. Her hair is long and she pulls it up, mostly, but definitely not in an old-fashioned way. Aunt Beverly likes loose clothing—styles that are "easy to move around in," she says—but even though that gives her a fairly casual appearance, almost all of her clothes are designer clothes. To me, she has a truly beautiful face—not a wrinkle at all and nearly flawless skin (except for one small scar that she got when she had the chicken pox as a little girl). She's got a great figure, although she's not really thin. I really can't think how else to describe her because I love her so much. And when you love someone, you don't always see her objectively. To me, she's the best aunt a girl could ever have. I guess I could tell you that she's thirty-four and has never been married, although I really can't understand why not, except that she's studied a lot and traveled a lot, and even lived in Europe for a while. The shop takes a lot of her time now, but she really seems to like it. And so do I. I'm going to work there part time this summer and I can hardly wait.

In addition to the people in our family, we have a dog named Scooter and a cat named Smithsonian. Scooter is a terrier and he's always on the move. Smithsonian is the laziest cat in the world. Dad calls her an institution because of the way she settles in by the fireplace and doesn't move for hours at a time.

And then there's Mom. Mom's name was Elizabeth Anna Stone Weber. She died in an automobile accident last year—her car was hit by a drunk driver. It's the easiest thing in the world for me to talk about my mother, and also the most difficult thing. I miss her beyond what words can tell. My mother was smart, very pretty with light brown curly hair, and she loved Dad, Kiersten, and me with all her heart. She was a musician and an artist. One of the things I miss most is Mom's singing around the house. She had a beautiful soprano voice and she knew all the songs—the old-timey ones and also modern ones. Dad used to call her a walking concert. She could sing anything.

The day that Mom died was the saddest day in my life. I can't imagine that any day in the future will be sadder. It felt like a giant gaping hole opened up in my heart. And when I think about Mom now—even though it's almost a year ago that she died—I still feel like crying. Then I'll remember something funny that she said or did, and I feel like laughing. Sometimes I just laugh and cry at the same time.

It was Mom's death that caused us to make the move to Collinsville. Kiersten and I had lived at Eagle Point, on the bay, all our lives until now. That's when Grandpa Stone invited Dad to come to Collinsville and work with him as his partner in the hardware store. Mom was Grandpa's only child and Grandma Stone died when I was just a little girl. So, Grandpa Stone said to Dad, "I want to leave the hardware store to family. You're the only son I have. You and Katelyn and Kiersten are my only family. Why don't you come to Collinsville?" Dad had been working as a building contractor in Eagle Point, but building has been slow lately, so he decided to take Grandpa up on his offer. Plus, he wanted us to be able to get to know Grandpa better. Plus, he wanted us to have the chance to be around Aunt Beverly on a daily basis. Kiersten and I were happy about that. Aunt Beverly has always been like a second mother to us.

It's really rather unusual that Aunt Beverly is in Collinsville, where Grandpa Stone lives. Aunt Beverly and Mom were friends in college—McKinney College, to be exact. Aunt Beverly came to Collinsville for visits with Mom several times when they were college students, and about four years ago when Aunt Beverly quit her job in the city and went into business for herself, she decided she liked Collinsville better than any other place she had visited, so she moved here. I remember her saying to us, "I have lots of good memories of Collinsville, so I think I'll make some more." Aunt Beverly calls herself a memory-maker. She sometimes calls Kiersten and me and says, "Let's make a memory"—and we've come to realize that when she says that, we're about to have a fun experience together! Aunt Beverly is the one who introduced Mom and Dad to each other—she told us one time that she's not only a memory-maker, but a great matchmaker and that she's already on the lookout for husbands for Kiersten and me. I told her she'd have to look a long, long time for me.

I'm not much into boys. My friends in Eagle Point were absolutely wild about boys. I guess I've never met a boy I really liked all that much.

Which sorta brings us back to what happened

at noon today. You see, ever since we've moved to Collinsville, I have felt like a fish out of water. We actually moved to this house about three weeks ago—it took us awhile to pack up our things in Eagle Point. And then we unpacked for about a week before we started school. Dad said when we moved, "I think it would be a good idea for you girls to attend school for the last few weeks of the term in Collinsville. That way, you'll get to know some of the kids before summer and you won't be starting out as strangers next fall." I'm sure it seemed like a good idea at the time, but from where I sit today, I'm not so sure. I think it would have been a lot better to finish out the year with my friends in Eagle Point. There's not much I can do about that now, though.

All the kids at Collinsville High School have been friends all year, and it's been really tough to try to get to know people. Everybody has their little clique. It's as if they've all put down roots into the school, and nobody seems to see me as a person who also has roots.

When I stop to think about it, I have *deep* roots in Collinsville. Stone's Hardware has been around forever, and I have an aunt who owns a shop here and I've visited here several times a year ever since I was born. But nobody seems to associate Weber with Stone, or with the shop at 4th and Elm.

Then, too, the routine is a little different in

high school. In Eagle Point, our junior high included the ninth grade, which is what I'm in. Here in Collinsville, ninth grade is the first year of high school. So I've gone from being at the top of the heap, so to speak, to the bottom. At Eagle Point, I really knew my way around the school, and I knew all the teachers. As Dad says, "I knew the ropes." Here at Collinsville, I'm not as sure of myself. I'm not even sure what it is that I *don't* know about being in high school. And I don't really like that feeling. Still, there's not much I can do about it except try to cope and try not to make any obvious mistakes that will cause everybody to laugh at me.

All of this probably sounds as if I've not met anybody at Collinsville High. That really isn't the case. I've met lots of people, learned lots of names, and am getting to know a little about a few people by watching the way they respond in class. The girls have been friendly enough—saying hello in the hall and asking me polite questions while we're waiting for gym class to begin. One group of girls asked me to sit with them at lunch one day, but then they talked about people I didn't know, so I really felt out of place. The next day, there wasn't an empty spot at their table, so I decided to take my sandwich and go outside. I wandered around the schoolyard a little bit and walked over into the park, and that's when I stum-

10

bled across the place where I've spent every noon hour since.

I found an old stone bench next to a little fountain in an out-of-the-way shady courtyard that's part of the park that's right next door to the oldest buildings of the high school. The courtyard seems very old fashioned and is about as far away from the Snack Shack as you can go and still be within earshot of the bell. Most of the kids hang around the Snack Shack, eat in the patio cafeteria, or stand around in the student parking lot at noon. Nobody seems to go over into the park.

I've been coming to Emily's Place for six days now, and I've never seen anybody else around. Each day, I have come to the park expecting to find someone in the courtyard. I've had my excuses and "excuse me's" all prepared in case I ran into someone, but the stone bench has always been empty. There's a little plaque at the base of the fountain that says "In memory of Emily, 1922–1940." That's why I call it Emily's Place.

Yesterday a girl named Alice asked me where I was going for lunch. I smiled and said, "Emily's Place." It made me feel as if I had a friend. I noticed that Alice looked at me in a little different way. It's almost as if she thought that I might make a better friend if I already *had* a friend named Emily! I felt like telling her that I also had a dozen other friends waiting for me, but I didn't.

In many ways, I feel that I do have a friend named Emily. I'd rather sit and read a good book and munch on an apple for a half hour in her courtyard, and try to imagine what she was like as a little girl and as a teen-ager like me, than make the effort to engage in small talk with people I may decide later that I don't like all that much. I've just about decided that the best I can hope for is to endure the next four weeks and try to make a friend or two this summer.

I've also faced the possibility that I may not make any friends at Collinsville High School. That isn't a great thought, but it could be reality. I know I'm not really the high school type.

Now before you jump to any conclusions, let me explain a little bit. People have always told me that I act older than my age. I think that's because I read a lot and Mom and Dad always talked to Kiersten and me as if we could understand the issues and the topics they wanted to discuss. Grandpa Stone said one time that "everybody has a blossoming time." I asked him what he meant and he said, "There comes a time when people just come into their own. They feel at home in the world, no matter where they are." That didn't make a whole lot of sense to me when he said it, but I think I'm beginning to understand a little more now. I'm looking forward to that time in my life, and I have a hunch it's going to be when I'm a college girl.

I have always wanted to be a college girl. When I was little, I'd watch the college girls at church and think, *I'd like to be just like them.* They all seemed so self-confident and they laughed a lot and talked easily with one another. I used to love to listen to Mom and Aunt Beverly talk about the times when they were at McKinney College. I dreamed of having a friend like Mom or Aunt Beverly when I went there—somebody I can really trust and share everything with.

Very specifically, I have always intended to be a McKinney College girl—at least until today. I've daydreamed a lot about McKinney in just the last couple of weeks—how I'd change the way I look, completely! And how I'd know what to say and do to meet other college students. And how I'd feel self-confident that this was "my time" to blossom. Collinsville High just may be a stage I need to endure. And even though it's three long years, I'm sure I can do it. McKinney College is ahead! And, of course, *nobody* would know me there. It would be a one hundred percent fresh start—my time to blossom, without interference, without a "past" to haunt me.

So, you see, Journal, I had just about decided that I wasn't going to worry about making new friends this spring—or maybe even ever—at CHS.

In fact, I'd just about decided that McKinney College would be the real "starting point" of my life, and that these next three years would be years for reading and working in the bookshop and spending time with Grandpa and Aunt Beverly.

I hadn't counted at all on having someone come up behind me while I was sitting in Emily's Place, very deep into *Green Dolphin Street* by Elizabeth Gouge—an absolutely fabulous book, by the way—and imagining myself thousands of miles away in the wilderness of New Zealand. I certainly hadn't counted on that person saying "I hear you're going to McKinney."

Those six words brought me back to the present and to Collinsville High School with a most unwelcome jolt.

Who could possibly know about McKinney?

Why would somebody be saying that to me, invading my private thoughts and coming into Emily's Place totally uninvited?

Was I hearing things?

Wouldn't a normal person say something like "Hello," or "Oh, excuse me for interrupting you," or "Do you mind if I join you?" if they just came up on someone reading a book in an ever-so-private little courtyard with a fountain?

And then . . . worst of the worst . . . I turned around to find Jon Weaver standing in the entrance to the courtyard. He was grinning like a Cheshire cat, as if he was actually expecting me to say something in reply.

Which I couldn't do, of course.

It's very difficult to be civil to a person—much less a *boy*—who has just waltzed into your secret dreams and turned them upside down without so much as an apology for being rude.

I picked up my pack and my book as quickly as I could and walked past Jon Weaver without saying a word and without even looking in his direction. I pretended he was invisible. I think he may even have had to jump back a bit to get out of my way.

One thing about me—I can walk in a very determined way. And that's just what I did, all the way back to the halls of the school. Fortunately for me, the bell rang just as I got to the door of my history classroom. I really don't remember much about history, or English. I tried to work out my frustration in phys ed class. I even did an extra set of sit-ups. All I could think about, though, was getting home.

Chapter Two

Things Get Worse

J remember Gramma Weber telling me when I was only about six or seven, "Sometimes, little Katie, things get worse before they get better." At the time, I had crawled up on Gramma's lap and we were praying together that a thunderstorm would stop. I couldn't understand why the claps of thunder only grew louder the more we prayed. God always seemed to answer Gramma's prayers right away, especially the ones she prayed about my skinned knees and lost hair ribbons. I've realized since then that Gramma's words apply to a lot more than rain storms. As a matter of fact, Journal, that's exactly what happened today. Things got worse.

After I wrote in you last night, I started to think, *Just how could Jon Weaver have found out that I was thinking about going to McKinney College?*

I don't talk much about McKinney College, at least not with anyone other than Aunt Beverly. Even then, it's not something we talk about every day, or even every week. I don't even remember the last time we had a serious talk about college! Anyway, Aunt Beverly has been on her buying trip for more than a week, so she couldn't possibly be the one who had talked to Jon Weaver about McKinney.

Kiersten knows that I want to go to McKinney someday. She wants to go there, too. But she's only ten and I can't imagine that she has given McKinney a single thought since we've moved to Collinsville. Unlike me, Kiersten has already made lots of friends here, especially a girl named Mari, who is a year younger than Kiersten. Mari is half Chinese and cute as a button with her long straight dark hair, thick bangs, and rose-rimmed glasses. She and Kiersten seem to be able to giggle by the hour, about little or nothing. Mari does have an older sister named Kim that Kiersten has talked about a couple of times, but I've never met her, and it's a real stretch to think that Kiersten may have told Kim who might have told Jon Weaver. I've never seen Jon Weaver talking to anybody.

How is it that I know Jon Weaver's name? Well,

17

he sits directly in front of me in homeroom, first period, and also in my algebra class, second period. In both classes, the teacher has made us sit in alphabetical order, and since his name is Weaver and my last name is Weber, there you have it. I sit directly behind him in both classes.

That certainly doesn't mean that I *know* him. Mostly I know the back of his head. Perhaps the best thing I can say for him is that he combs his hair, unlike some of the boys at Collinsville High School. I don't have anything against long hair or unusual styles, mind you, but I've never really understood a guy not putting a comb through his hair before he comes to school. Jon Weaver's hair is dark brown and rather straight. He's about medium height for a guy, I guess. Average looking, I guess. Nothing that really stands out. I have noticed that he wears button-down shirts, which nobody else in the school seems to wear. (Dad and Grandpa do, but they don't count as fashion experts! Mom was forever trying to get both of them to try new styles, but Dad and Grandpa would just smile at her suggestions and wink at each other when she wasn't looking.)

Jon Weaver nearly always makes it to homeroom on time, although sometimes he slides into his seat just as the bell rings. He cuts it pretty close on most days. Which is fine with me. I don't

18

have to worry about him turning around and trying to start a conversation.

Jon Weaver has answered a couple of pretty tough questions in algebra class and he always has his algebra homework done, so I guess he must be pretty smart. Algebra isn't my best subject by a long shot, so I don't really know if he's all-around *smart*, or just smarter than I am in math. I'd know more if he was in my English class, but he isn't.

Come to think of it, I hardly ever see Jon Weaver in the halls as we change classes. His schedule must be a lot different from mine. And I've never heard anybody call him anything other than Jon Weaver. Maybe that's because I've only heard Mr. Grassmyer, who is our homeroom teacher as well as the algebra teacher, call him by name. Surely he doesn't go by his full name all the time?

Anyway . . . I've rambled from my subject, which was the time I spent last night trying to figure out just how Jon Weaver might have known about McKinney College. I fussed and fumed about it for more than an hour and then, as I was rolling over on my big four-poster bed, I glanced toward my nightstand and there I saw it—the new catalog for McKinney College. My mind immediately raced back to last Friday, when I had picked up the catalog from the school counselor's office. I had gone into the CHS library right after school on Thursday to see if I could find a new McKinney catalog—mine is two years old and I know they change the catalogs from time to time—and the librarian had told me that the college catalogs were in the school counselor's office.

So . . . at the start of my lunch period on Friday, I went into the counselor's office and found that she had one entire little room filled with shelves that had nothing but college catalogs. A computer was on a table in the center of the room. A nice woman—she is probably the school counselor, although she never introduced herself that way—told me that her name was Miss Kattenhorn and she explained to me that the computer was used for taking aptitude tests, in order to help students discover their talents and to explore areas in which they might like to work after college. I told Miss Kattenhorn that I already knew what I wanted to do after college, but that I'd like to check out one of the college catalogs. She asked me which one. I said, "McKinney College." She helped me find it, fill out the check-out card, and that was that.

All the pieces seemed to come together as I thought back over that encounter. Miss Kattenhorn must have been the one! She was the only person who knew that I was interested in going to McKinney. Jon Weaver must have overheard us talking, or maybe Miss Kattenhorn had told him later that a girl named Katelyn Weber was thinking about going to McKinney.

Either way, I felt angry and betrayed when I put all the pieces together. The more I thought about it as I bathed and brushed my teeth last night, the more upset I became. I brushed my hair so hard it almost hurt.

How dare Jon Weaver eavesdrop? *If he had.*

How dare Miss Kattenhorn tell someone else my private business? *If she did.*

I made a decision before I climbed into bed that when I returned the catalog, I was going to tell Miss Kattenhorn to mind her own affairs and leave mine alone. And with that, I also decided to take the catalog back today—after all, if I can't go there now and really make McKinney College my fresh start in life, why look at the catalog?

So, Journal, I walked—in my most determined way—toward the counselor's office at the start of the lunch period today. I pulled out my card to check in the catalog and then as I was going toward the shelf to put it back in its rightful place—just as Miss Kattenhorn had explained I should do—I saw Jon Weaver. He was sitting at the computer, which was between us, so I hadn't seen him as I walked into the room. He was looking right at me, with that same Cheshire-style grin, as if he knew the punch line to a joke I hadn't heard. Needless to say, I was startled to see him there. He could have had the courtesy to clear his throat or say hello or something when I came in. He didn't need to wait until I was surprised! *He really is a strange one,* I thought. All in all, however, I think I recovered fairly well.

I put the McKinney College catalog on the table next to him and said, "Here's the McKinney catalog if you're so interested in going there."

"Who said I wanted to go there?" Jon Weaver said in a fairly matter-of-fact tone of voice, although he had a big grin on his face.

"Well, don't you?" I asked. I was so surprised at what he said that I couldn't think of anything really clever to say back.

"Not necessarily. I really don't know that much about McKinney College. Is it a good school?"

If he didn't know about it, how did he know I knew about it? I had to get to the bottom of this. . . .

"Then how did you know I was interested in going to McKinney College?" I put heavy emphasis on *was.*

"I came in to check out a couple of aptitude-testing books earlier this week and when I went to the file of check-out cards, I saw your name and card. After all, you're name is immediately *after* mine alphabetically. Or maybe you hadn't noticed . . ." I couldn't really tell if he was teasing or putting me down. Either way, I felt irritated. Does he ever say *anything* without that silly smile on his face?

"Yeah, I noticed," I said.

At that point Miss Kattenhorn walked into the little room and asked if she could help us. We both said no, and I left the room as quickly as I could. Come to think of it, I never did put that catalog back on the shelf. I hope Jon Weaver did, but then again . . . I guess I should go back tomorrow—well, on Monday, at least—to make sure it got back to the slot where it belongs. It's not like me to leave things at loose ends. Dad sometimes laughs when he says, "Kat-kat"—that's one of his nicknames for me—"you never leave *anything* until all the details are tied down." He thinks that trait in me would make me a better journalist than a novelist. I'm not convinced, and frankly I am not at all interested in being a newspaper reporter.

So, Journal, I didn't get to give my very well crafted speech to Miss Kattenhorn. I was really looking forward to an adult-to-adult talk with her about the need for honoring another person's privacy, even if that other person was a high school freshman. On the other hand, I probably wouldn't have had the nerve to say what I really wanted to say. I also know that Jon Weaver wasn't eavesdropping, so I really have no business being upset with him.

Which makes me think that I was really making much ado about nothing—one of my favorite lines from Shakespeare, by the way. I have this nagging feeling that I ought to apologize to Jon Weaver, but I can't really nail down why I feel that way. He was the one who interrupted my peaceful lunch hour yesterday, and he was the one who had spied on my check-out card last week. Still, I may have been a little rude to him. And all in all, I know I'm making a big deal out of very little. So what if he's weird? So what if I've happened to bump into him a couple of times? Why do I care what he thinks or does? Why does he care what I check out, or where I go to college?

All of this is very confusing, Journal. And I can't seem to sort it out very well. That's probably a good clue that I should quit writing and go to sleep.

Before I do . . . shall I describe for you where it is that you spend the night? There's a little piece of furniture by my bed that has a small drawer at the top and then a door below it that opens to a space with two shelves. I call it my nightstand, but Aunt Beverly says it's an antique "commode," whatever that means. On the bottom shelf, I keep a box of special things, and you. The shelf is deep enough that in front of it, I can put an extra set of sheets and pillow cases. That's in case anybody goes snooping—meaning, of course, Kiersten.

Kiersten has a room of her own, right next to mine, and that eliminates a big hassle. Plus, now that she's ten, she doesn't snoop nearly as much as she used to. In Eagle Point, we shared a room and no matter how hard I tried, I could hardly ever keep things private. Kiersten especially liked to snoop around until she found my stories. I don't think it was the stories she liked as much as she enjoyed making me upset. As much as I'd tell her that a writer doesn't like for her work to be read "in progress"—a term Mom taught me—it didn't seem to matter to Kiersten.

I like my room here in Collinsville a lot. We have a big two-story house that Dad says is sixty years old. The bedrooms are on the top floor. My room is wallpapered in a pattern that is mostly yellow, with tiny pink flowers and little green vines scattered on it, and my bedspread is white. I have an old walnut desk by the window. It looks out on the front lawn and the big oak tree. Some of the branches of the oak tree come right next to my bedroom window, so when I'm sitting at my desk, it's easy for me to imagine that I'm in my own little tree house. I have lace curtains at the windows—lacier than the ones I had in my room back in Eagle Point. I also have a big overstuffed chair in my room and an old-fashioned floor lamp with a pleated shade. The chair—which is big enough so that I really can curl up with a book—is also covered with yellow flowers, but not in the same pattern as the wallpaper. It all goes together pretty well, though. Aunt Beverly calls it the "pattern on pattern" look. I have a hooked rug in yellow, gray, white, and pink on the floor and some embroidered pillows on my bed. Mom made the rug and the pillows, so they are extra special to me.

I know I told you earlier that I'm not the floral type—and it's true that I don't have any dresses with flowers on them—but this room makes me happy and reminds me of Mom and the flower garden she grew every spring in the big clay pots on our deck. The chair was one she had in her bedroom back in Eagle Point.

I like to keep my room neat, unlike Kiersten. If she had a journal, she'd never have to worry about my finding it. Her room is always in such an uproar that she can hardly find her bed. Gramma Weber calls her a pack rat, but she means it in a nice way. Gramma calls *herself* a pack rat, too.

Speaking of Gramma, I just remembered the rest of Gramma's phrase: "Sometimes, little Katie, things get worse before they get better . . . but God always answers prayer."

I wonder if God could sort out all this mess with Jon Weaver. I really would like to go to McKinney College for a fresh start someday, and the more I think about it, I'd like to make some friends here, too. Maybe I should pray about it.

Chapter Three

Strange
Twists

*W*ell, dear Journal, God certainly has a strange
sense of humor sometimes.

Do you think I'm irreverent for saying that? I
suspect some people might think so, but I don't
mean it in an irreverent way. God surely must
have a sense of humor—just look at all the funny
things He made. Plus, He gave us the ability to
laugh. I think He probably enjoys playing a joke
on us now and then. Anyway . . . I feel as if He
played one on me today.

It's been two days since I've written in you, so
perhaps I should describe Saturday a little. It was
actually a rather glorious day. Aunt Beverly came
home from her buying trip late Friday night, so
she was at the bookshop early on Saturday morning. I knew she'd be there, so I got up extra early

and as soon as breakfast was over, I raced down to the shop to see her. As usual, she greeted me with a big hug and a smile. I don't think I'll ever get too old for Aunt Beverly's hugs. She's just the hugging type—or so she says.

Anyway, Aunt Beverly had lots to tell me about the things she had ordered for the shop, and we also had several boxes of books to unpack—shipments that came while she was away. I helped her put them on the shelves in alphabetical order, and also helped her make a new display for the front window, showing some of the latest titles.

There isn't anything that I don't like about Aunt Beverly's bookshop. She calls it "The Wonderful Life Shop." We've talked about the name a lot so I know just what it means to her. In the first place, she loves that old movie, *It's a Wonderful Life*—the one starring Jimmy Stewart that everybody seems to play a dozen times during the Christmas season. Aunt Beverly has a black-and-white poster from the movie hanging in one corner of the shop.

Aunt Beverly also says that she believes in the message of the movie: that every life is important and has a wonderful meaning, when viewed from God's perspective. Aunt Beverly has a lot of books about God in her shop, but her shop isn't just a Christian bookstore, or even just a bookstore, for that matter. All of the books she has are books that she says have a "wonderful" message—books that are beautiful to look at, well-written, and have stories that are good for people of all ages to read. A lot of her books are what Grandpa calls the classics.

Beyond the books, Aunt Beverly has lots of things that relate to writing—such as little lap desks, unusual pens, ink wells, old-fashioned blotters. She has a couple of antique typewriters, and several old leather-bound accounting books. I tell her nearly every time I'm in the shop, "Someday I want to own one of everything." Aunt Beverly always laughs and says back, "Then maybe someday you'll just have to own this shop!" It's not a bad idea, as far as I'm concerned.

Aunt Beverly also has teapots and teacups, old lace tablecloths, lots of bells—old and new. After all, a "Wonderful Life" store should have some bells to ring! She also has some pretty vases. Even though they are for sale, Aunt Beverly keeps them filled with flowers. One area of the wall where the old-style cash register is located has lots of different kinds of stationery that a person can mix and match. Another part of the wall is lined with lots of different teas, candies, and coffees. Aunt Beverly always has a pot of tea or coffee brewing so that the customers can have a cup to drink as they browse through the shop.

Dad says Aunt Beverly makes good money in

the shop, but it wouldn't matter to me if she never sold anything. I just love going in, sitting down, and taking it all in—the smells, the sound of the grandfather clock ticking in the corner, the look of all the beautiful things, the faces of the customers, who always seem to leave a little happier than when they come in. I can hardly wait for summer to come so I can work with Aunt Beverly every day.

As we were unpacking some of the books, I told Aunt Beverly about buying you, Journal. As I suspected, she gave you to me as a gift.

I also told Aunt Beverly about Jon Weaver, although I never told her his name. She didn't say anything at first and then she said, "I think he's trying to be your friend."

I must admit, that thought never entered my mind. "Why would he want to be my friend?" I asked her.

Aunt Beverly said, "Nobody really knows what makes one person want to be friends with another person. The trouble is, most people who would like to be friends with others don't really know how to go about it. They sometimes dance all around each other and never do connect."

At that point, a customer came in and Aunt Beverly waited on him. He was a tall man wearing an old-fashioned golf cap. I couldn't see him very clearly but his voice sounded nice and he and Aunt

Beverly both laughed a couple of times. Aunt Beverly helped him pick out three books and a pound of decaffeinated Swiss Almond coffee—two of the books were ones that we had just unpacked. While she waited on him, I took some of the empty boxes out into the alleyway.

The customer was gone when I went back into the store. Aunt Beverly picked up our conversation where she had left off. "The real question, Katelyn, is 'Would you like to be friends with this boy?'" she asked.

"I'm not in the market right now for a *boy-friend*," I said. "No matchmaking yet!"

"That's not what I mean," Aunt Beverly said. "I meant just as a friend. It's possible to have a friend who's a guy, and to know a guy who's just a friend—right?"

"I don't know. I haven't really thought about it."

"Well, is there something about this boy that you'd like to know?"

"I'm sorta interested in knowing why he was taking an aptitude test on the computer, I guess. I'd like to know about the test and what he found out and whether he thinks the test is a good one for helping a person."

"Then . . . ask him!" Aunt Beverly said.

"You mean, just walk up and say, 'Hi, I want

to know about that computer'?" I laughed. "I can't see that happening, Aunt Beverly."

"Who knows?" she said. "Wait to see if you have a chance to talk to him again, and if you do, you can bring it up." She sounded very matter-of-fact about it, but somehow I sensed that her thoughts were elsewhere.

"Is there somebody that *you'd* like to get to know better, Aunt Beverly?"

"Yes, sneaky, I guess there is. You caught me daydreaming, didn't you?"

"Well, you did sorta have that far-away look in your eye. Who *i-i-i-i-i-is* he?" I teased.

"Actually, Katelyn, I'd like to get to know a little better that man who was just in here. The one who bought the three books and pound of coffee."

"Has he been in before?" I asked her. This was the most interesting thing I had heard all morning!

"Oh, a few times. He first came in about three or four weeks ago, and he seems to come in every few days for something. I'm beginning to think he might be interested in more than books and coffee."

"What are you going to do?" I asked eagerly.

"I think I'm going to ask him the next time he comes in, 'Have you ever taken an aptitude test on a computer, sir?'" Aunt Beverly laughed at her own clever idea.

"What's his name?" I asked. "Has he ever given you a check or a credit card so you could find out his name?"

"Yes, as a matter of fact, he did. His name is Clark Weaver."

"Clark Weaver!" You can imagine how stunned I was at that! "Oh, Aunt Beverly, the name of the boy I've been telling you about is Jon Weaver!"

"Oh, no!" Aunt Beverly said. We both had a big laugh over that. Could it be that they are related? We have no way of knowing. One thing Aunt Beverly said has me extra curious—she said that Clark Weaver had only been coming into the store for the last few weeks. Could it be that Jon Weaver is also a new kid at Collinsville High School?

No sooner had we stopped laughing than Kiersten and Mari came rushing into the shop. An older, very pretty girl followed them.

"Hi, Aunt Beverly," bubbled Kiersten. "Can we have a chocolate drop . . . p-l-e-a-s-e!" Aunt Beverly is always generous in giving Kiersten candy, but usually only one piece per visit. She said, "Sure, kiddo. And what about you, Mari? Do you want a chocolate drop, or perhaps something else today?" Mari scrunched up her face for a minute and then said, "I think I'd rather have a peppermint."

"One peppermint it is, then," said Aunt Beverly as she picked out one piece of candy from each jar and placed each in a separate little bag that had "The Wonderful Life Shop" printed on it.

"Is this lovely young lady with you girls?" Aunt Beverly asked, nodding toward the girl who had followed them in the store. "Yes," said Kiersten. "This is Kim! She's Mari's big sister. She likes candy, too."

"That's OK," said Kim, seeming to apologize a bit for Kiersten's enthusiasm.

"I'd love to give you a piece of your choice," said Aunt Beverly. "Any friend of Kiersten's is a friend of mine."

Kim looked at all the jars and finally settled on a caramel chew.

"Oh," said Aunt Beverly as she picked out the biggest piece she could find and put it in the little sack, "you like the same kind of candy as my niece Katelyn."

"Hi," I said, popping my head out from behind the bookshelf where I had been moving a few books down to make room for the new titles. "My name is Katelyn."

At long last, I met Kim. She was really easy to talk to, and while Aunt Beverly showed some of her new purchases to Kiersten and Mari, Kim and I talked about school. I found out that she's also in ninth grade, but that she has been going to a private Christian school that's part of Faith Community Fellowship, which is just a couple of miles from our house. Kim invited me to meet her at church on Sunday and said she was glad to find another ninth-grader who lived so close to her. It seems most of the kids in her school live on the other side of town.

I also found out that her name is actually Kimberly. She told me that the kids at school call her Kimber, and that her family calls her Kimmie. Only Kiersten calls her Kim! "That's just like Kiersten," I said. "She always finds a detour if there's one to take."

And then I added, "What would you like for me to call you?"

"Kimber would be just fine," she said.

Well . . . that's the first half of the story, Journal. I suppose we could call it the Saturday saga. Sunday was a whole day unto itself.

I talked to Dad on Saturday night about the possibility of Kiersten and me going with Mari and Kimber to church, and he thought it was a great idea. In fact, he decided to come along. Back in Eagle Point, we went to church every Sunday, but since moving to Collinsville, we hadn't been to a church yet. There just seemed to be so much settling in to do with the move, plus Grandpa and Dad had been taking turns helping out at Aunt Beverly's shop while she was away on her buying trip. Grandpa goes to the First Baptist Church that's downtown, but I overheard Dad say that he didn't think he'd be able to go there. He and Mom were married in that church and Dad thought it would bring back too many memories to go there right now. Grandpa seemed to understand, and he had actually recommended Faith Community Fellowship to Dad. So it seemed like the right thing to do.

On Sunday morning, we made it to church in plenty of time and we spotted Kimber and Mari right away, so we sat with them and their parents, Dr. and Mrs. Chan. Dad found out that Dr. Chan is a dentist, and Dr. Chan discovered that Dad could probably help him with his new office computer. Dad's a whiz at computers. He used one in his building business before we moved and now he's setting up a computer program for Stone's Hardware.

The service was a really neat one. I liked all the praise songs they sang at the start of the service. They were easy to learn and easy to sing. Then the minister said, "Now, turn around and say 'God bless you' to everybody around you." Kimber and I said "God bless you" to each other, and so did Kiersten and I. Then I turned around, and you wouldn't believe it . . . Jon Weaver was standing directly behind me!

"Hi," he said, with that same old grin. "I thought I'd see what it was like to sit behind *you* instead of you sitting behind me."

"God bless you, Jon Weaver," I said. And decided to throw in a smile for good measure.

"God bless *you*," said Jon Weaver. And then he added, "And you can call me just Jon."

"OK, just Jon," I said. He grimaced, and suddenly I felt the score was even between us. I had finally caught him off guard, too.

I don't really remember much about the rest of the service. After it was over, I turned around to see if Jon Weaver was still behind us so I could introduce Kimber to him, but he was already on his way out. I didn't see anyone with him that looked like Mr. Clark Weaver. The one thing I did hear during the service was an invitation to the young people there to come to a special service at six o'clock on Sunday evening. Kimber asked me, "Would you like to go to the youth group meeting tonight?"

I asked, "Are you going?"

"I'd like to," she said. "Some of the kids who are in my school go, but not all of them. And then there are some kids who come to youth group who aren't in the school. None of my close friends from school go on a regular basis, though, so I sometimes feel alone and a little out of place. I know you probably haven't noticed, but I'm really kinda shy. I'd like it if we could go together."

"Sure!" I said. "And no, I hadn't noticed that you're shy."

I think, Journal, that I just may have found a friend in Kimber.

On to the final act of this three-part saga: Sunday night at youth group! Kimber and I went and we had a great time. The speaker was the youth pastor, Bert Brown. He and his wife, Sharyn, are youth co-pastors and they both are really nice. Sharyn sang and taught us a couple of new songs. Bert talked about emotions, and about how we need to learn to channel our emotions in the right way so we don't hurt other people or ourselves. What he said made a lot of sense. I had never really thought about how much we base what we say and do on our feelings, and how we can hurt ourselves if we keep a lot of anger or bitterness locked up inside.

We met in a basement room that was called the Fellowship Hall, and there were about thirty kids in all—from seventh grade to twelfth grade. Kimber introduced me to a boy and a girl from her school. Although I didn't see him before the meeting started, I saw Jon Weaver walking toward the door after the service. I called to him and when he saw me, I waved for him to come over to our little group. I introduced him to Kimber and to the other two kids and we talked for a minute or two. Jon said he had to leave and when Kimber and I looked at our watches, we knew that we did, too, if we were going to meet Dr. Chan at the time we promised. I can't remember much of what we said in those few moments. The only thing that I really remember is that when Kimber asked Jon Weaver how long he had lived in Collinsville, Jon replied, "We just moved here last month."

It's true, Journal. Jon Weaver is a new kid, just like me! We just may have enough in common to become friends after all. I can't help wondering what his relationship might be to a guy named Clark! Yes, I definitely have some things I'd like to find out about Jon Weaver.

Chapter Four

Uncommon Commonalities

Friday
7 P.M.

*W*hat a week!

I realize I haven't written in you, Journal, for several days now. Life has been very busy—with friends! That's something I could hardly have imagined a week ago.

I have two major things to tell you.

The first is an update on Jon. After what happened over the weekend, I wasn't surprised when Jon arrived at school on Monday morning thirty seconds *before* the bell rang, a record for him. That was long enough for him to turn around and say, "Good morning, Miss Weber. I trust you slept well last night" . . . and for me to respond, "Good morning, Mr. Weaver. I did, thank you."

Between classes I tried what Aunt Beverly had

suggested. I asked him, "Did you finish the aptitude test in Miss Kattenhorn's office?"

"Yes," Jon said. "It told me what I already knew, for the most part."

"What was that?" I asked.

"Oh," Jon said with his usual grin, "that I'm good at the things I really like to do."

"What are those things?" I was actually rather surprised that I wanted to know, but I did.

"Computers. Science. Math. The usual nerd things. Not exactly the profile of the All-American kid that I know I am."

By that time we had arrived at algebra class.

"There's nothing wrong with computers," I said. "My dad is really good at computers."

"Really?" Jon asked. He seemed genuinely interested.

"Yes. He's developing a major inventory system for our family hardware store, and when he was a building contractor, he did some design work and engineering on computers."

"Maybe I could talk to him sometime. My dad isn't into computers at all. He'd rather read a book or play golf."

I was a bit upset when the bell rang that it was time for class to begin. It was easy to talk to Jon. In fact, it was as easy as talking to any friend I've ever had.

When algebra class was over, Jon said, "What are you doing after school?"

"Going home, I guess. I don't have any major plans."

"Would you like to take a look at that aptitude program in Miss Kattenhorn's room?" he asked. "I've figured out some shortcuts to it."

"Sure," I said. I wasn't quite ready to let Jon Weaver know that I had already figured out what I want to do with my life.

So . . . Journal . . . that's how it happened that Jon and I were late leaving school on Monday afternoon. We spent an hour in the school counselor's office, with Jon showing me how to speed through the answers on the aptitude test. I made it through about half of the program before Miss Kattenhorn came in to tell us that it was time for the "career lab" to close. Jon and I just looked at each other, and then we burst out laughing. We had no idea we had been in a *lab* of any kind!

As we walked away from the school toward Elm Street, Jon fell into step with me and I realized that he was planning to walk me home. "You don't need to walk me home," I said. "I only live a couple of blocks away."

"I know," he said. "You live at Three-Twenty-Five Maple. I've seen you on your porch."

I wasn't quite sure what to say. *What more had Jon Weaver spied out about my life?* Then he went on to say, "I live at Five-Twenty-Five Maple, just two blocks up the street. I have to walk by your house on my way home anyway."

I felt a little relieved. Maybe Jon wasn't a spy as much as he was just very observant. I was glad for the company.

That is, until a car rounded the corner and seemed to speed directly toward us! We both jumped back away from the curb, off the sidewalk and onto the lawn, as the car skidded into a big puddle of water next to the curb, and then spun around one hundred and eighty degrees as the driver slammed on the brakes with a very loud squeal. I didn't get any water on me, but Jon was pretty drenched. As the car started to spin its wheels and then speed back up the street in the direction from which it had come, two of the guys in the car stuck their heads out of the windows and yelled, "Hey, weevil!"

I was angry. No, indignant is a better word. How dare they do that without any repercussion?

"Friends of yours?" I asked, trying to lighten the mood as Jon picked up his books and tried to wipe the muddy water off them.

"Hardly," Jon said.

"Do you know them at all?" I asked. I could tell that Jon was not only angry—and trying hard to control his anger—but he was a little embarrassed. "Who *are* they?" When Jon hesitated a minute, I felt a little guilty. I knew I had sounded like I was conducting an inquisition. "I'm sorry," I said. "I didn't mean to sound so much like a parole officer. I just don't particularly like it when someone calls a friend of mine a weevil."

That brought the grin back to Jon's face. "Short for Weaver, I think," he said.

"Not a particularly great nickname," I said. "I think I could come up with something better."

"Really?" Jon said with his grin in full force by now. "I'd like to hear it."

"I'll give it a think," I said, "and let you know when I come up with something. I really don't know you all that well."

We walked on for a little way in silence and then Jon said, "They're in my computer class."

"Oh?"

"Yeah. They really don't have a clue as to what is going on, and like I told you this morning, computers are something I'm really good at. I guess they don't like the fact that the teacher seems to spend some extra time and attention at my work station."

"Why should they care? Are they asking for extra help?"

"Not really asking for extra help. More like asking for extra attention. The teacher is Miss Scaroni, and she's the only reason these guys are in the class. She's really a knockout. Italian beauty, you know. These guys just hadn't counted on her also being a brain."

I wasn't sure in that moment that I liked the sound of Miss Scaroni spending a lot of time at Jon Weaver's computer work station, either, although I really can't understand, now that I think about it, why I should feel that way about a person I've never met, and who sounds like a real expert. For the most part, I've always liked to be around people who really know what they are doing.

"Thanks for caring that my name was defamed," Jon said as we got to my house.

"That's what friends are for," I said as I walked into the house.

Friends. Can you believe it, Journal? A week ago I could never have imagined it. Actually, four days ago it seemed like an impossibility! Life really has a way of taking strange turns.

On Tuesday, Jon and I finished the aptitude tests, and on Wednesday we got the results. "Well," Jon said. "It looks like you're good with words and facts—things like English, history, and languages, I take it?"

"Yeah," I admitted. "That's the way it goes."

"Sounds like we're opposites," Jon said, and I couldn't tell if he was grinning or not.

"Yeah. Sounds like it."

"I'm glad," Jon said.

"You're *glad*? Why would you be glad?"

"Well," Jon went on, "maybe we can help each other. I can help you out in math and science if you need it, and you can help me in English, history, and Spanish."

"Not a bad idea," I said.

Oh . . .

I forgot to tell you, Journal. I ran into the four boys who were in that mud-slinging car as I was walking down the hall at the end of the day on Wednesday. It was a classic scene. I'm still chuckling over it two days later!

The guys were walking toward me as I rounded the corner. I stood in their way and said, "Are you the four very rude guys who have a crush on Miss Scaroni and are still learning to drive?"

One of them leaned toward me and said, "What's it to you, freshman?" Another one of the guys really got in my face and said, "S-o-o-o-o-o?"

"So I just wanted to make sure I could identify you guys in a line-up if I had to," I said. I couldn't believe I was so bold. Later, I shook for fifteen minutes at what I had said. But at the time, I felt like steel.

"Whoa," a third guy said, and at just that moment, Miss Scaroni put her head around the corner of the building and said, "Can I help you boys find the right words for a proper apology?"

You've never seen four more embarrassed juniors in your life! They pretty much turned and ran, although they tried to be cool about it. I'm sure I'm now on their enemy list right along with Jon, but somehow I don't think they'll do anything. I don't mind at all being on a hit list with my "friend."

Speaking of which . . . Thursday—yesterday— was the day when the second big event of the week happened. I made another new friend, in probably the least likely circumstance that I could ever have imagined.

I was sitting in homeroom when a girl walked into the class with the principal, Dr. Collins. "This is Elizabeth Webster," she announced to Mr. Grassmyer. "A transfer from Rolling Hills."

"Take a seat," said Mr. Grassmyer, and he pointed to the empty chair directly behind me. Weaver . . . Weber . . . Webster . . . she had managed to fall right into alphabetical line. I hadn't thought about it before, but Mr. Grassmyer was probably trying to do some kind of probability calculations in his head over the fact that his three most recent students all had names that began with "W."

"Elizabeth," he said gruffly. "Is that what you like to be called or do you prefer to go by another name?"

There was no response behind me, and then I noticed that a few of the students who were staring from the front part of the room were starting to smile.

Oh, no! I thought. I had a big sense of panic for this new girl.

"L-l-l-libby," she finally managed to say. And then, before I or anybody else knew what was happening, Elizabeth Webster—Libby—got up and ran from the classroom. *What a dreadful start,* I thought. It's hard enough being a new kid, without a major embarrassment like that in your first five minutes at a new school!

And then, to my absolute shock, Mr. Grassmyer said, "Go after her, Katelyn."

Me? Why me? Just because I was sitting one seat ahead of her didn't make me an expert in a situation like this. I looked quickly down at Jon and he didn't have a grin on his face. He looked wide-eyed and scared, which is exactly the way I felt.

"Go on, now. Find her and bring her back."

Jon told me later that after I left the room, Mr. Grassmyer spent several minutes giving a very harsh lecture to the class about how rude some of the students had been to a person who stuttered. *Good for him!* It didn't help me much, though.

By the time I got out of the room, I couldn't see Libby anywhere. I slowly walked up and down the halls, calling her name occasionally, but certainly not loud enough to get the attention of any teacher. Finally, the thought hit me. *The park!* That's where I would have headed. And sure enough, as I got to the edge of the park, I saw Libby spot me and take off in a direction I knew well. She headed straight for Emily's Place!

I knew I had her cornered, but even as I approached the secret little courtyard with its old stone bench and crumbling fountain, I had no idea what I was going to say.

I found her sitting on the bench, her head in her lap, sobbing. She wasn't making a lot of noise, but I knew she was crying hard from the way her shoulders moved up and down.

"I like to come here, too," I finally managed to say as I walked toward her and sat down. I put my hand on her shoulder and said, "My name is Katelyn Weber. That's Weber with one B. I'm new in this school, too."

"You are?" she managed to say. She hadn't stuttered at all. That seemed like a pretty good sign.

"I call this courtyard 'Emily's Place,'" I said as I pointed out the plaque at the base of the fountain. "I come here a lot to eat lunch."

Libby sniffed. She was trying hard to stop crying.

"It's tough to be a new kid," I continued. "I've only been here two weeks, so I know a little about how you feel."

"You don't st-st-st-st-utter," she said.

"No," I said and then added with a wry little

twist to my voice. "I just don't say anything. I'm so shy that I can't get out *any* sounds."

Libby looked up and said, "You're talking fine now."

"So are you!" I said. She looked at me in surprise and then we both grinned as we realized that we really did have something in common. We both could talk just fine if we were in the presence of someone we could trust!

"My mother's name was Elizabeth," I said. "She died last year."

"I'm s-s-s-sorry," Libby said, and I could tell that she really meant it.

"Me, too," I said. "It's been a hard year. But I think I'd like it if you would be my friend. It would be nice to have a friend who has the same name as my mom."

"I'd l-l-like that, too," said Libby, who had managed to stop crying and was wiping her eyes.

"Think we should head back?" I asked her.

"My eyes are all r-r-r-ed," she said.

"Got any sunglasses?" I asked.

She nodded yes and added, "In my p-p-purse."

"You can put them on when we get back into the room. It's about time for classes to change, so we can wait outside until the bell rings, then dash in and get your purse and sunglasses, and I'll help you find your next class. Do you know what it is?"

"Algebra," she said with a sigh.

"That's my second period, too. And you're in luck. Mr. Grassmyer is the teacher, so he won't have to ask you anything. He already knows your name!"

Libby smiled—actually, it was more like a sad grin. "Thanks, Katelyn," she said as she got up from the stone bench.

"You're welcome, Libby," I replied. "I'm glad for a friend."

Jon met us as we came back in the room, and as soon as Libby had put on her sunglasses, he stuck out his hand toward her. "Jon Weaver," he said. "Pleased to meet you, Libby." She smiled and shook Jon's hand.

"Jon's one of us," I said. "He's only been here a few weeks."

Jon nodded. "I'm good at science, math, and computers. Katelyn's specialties are English, Spanish, and history. You got any specialties?"

Libby smiled. "I make great sp-sp-sp-spaghetti," she said. "Great!" we both said at once. Somebody has to cook!

And that's the way the week went, Journal. Two friends! Plus Kimber at church. Things in Collins- ville are definitely looking up. I haven't thought about McKinney College very much at all this week—but I did, by the way, make sure that the catalog was filed correctly on the shelf in the career lab. Like I said before, I don't like loose ends.

Chapter Five

Upcoming Attractions

*A*unt Beverly! Aunt Beverly!" I probably shouldn't have been calling to Aunt Beverly so loudly this morning as I rushed into her shop. It never dawned on me that she might have a customer. I've really got to learn to control my enthusiasm.

Anyway . . . Aunt Beverly popped her head up from where she had been stooped over behind the counter and said in a very droll shopkeeper voice, "May I help you, ma'am?"

"Oh, Aunt Beverly, I'm so excited," I said as I leaned over to give her a hug.

"*That* conclusion never entered my head," Aunt Beverly said with a big smile. "What's up?"

"Two of the most exciting things that have ever

happened in my life—well, at least since last week."

"I see," said Aunt Beverly. "And just what might those two things be?"

"First, Dad said this morning that he has it all arranged and we are going back to Eagle Point next weekend so I can graduate with my class."

"Great!" said Aunt Beverly. "How did that come about?"

"Dad called the principal and the principal said it was fine for me to come back and walk through the line and get my diploma from Eagle Point Junior High! In fact, he said he was hoping that I'd come back for the big event. There's a reception afterward and then a party for the grads. Isn't that fantastic?"

"Sure is!"

"And there's more! The principal even told Dad that I had been chosen earlier in the year to receive one of the awards that are given at graduation. I was chosen Best English Student."

"Oh, honey, that's great," said Aunt Beverly. I got an extra hug, as you might imagine. "Although I must say, I'm not all that surprised." Sometimes I think that the whole world would be a better place if everybody had a personal fan like Aunt Beverly.

"So when do you leave?" she asked.

"Well, that's the possible glitch in the system,"

I said. "Dad says we need to leave on Friday morning so I can make a Friday afternoon rehearsal. The graduation is Friday night. And we won't be coming back until Saturday morning. Which means . . . I won't be able to work next Saturday. Is that OK?"

"Of course it is. A gal only graduates once from junior high," said Aunt Beverly. "In fact, I just may see if I can find someone to fill in at the shop for me on Friday and Saturday so I can go with you."

"Oh, that would be wonderful!"

"Funny thing is," Aunt Beverly said, "I've never heard you say anything about junior high graduation before this moment. I didn't know it was important to you."

"Well, I didn't really think there was any way I could go back for graduation, so I tried not to think about it. I guess I didn't realize how much it meant to me until Dad brought it up. But now that I know we're going, I can hardly wait. It will be great to see everyone again. And you know me . . . it will be tying up a loose end."

Aunt Beverly nodded in agreement. My Aunt Beverly and I are a lot alike in that department. She likes things done in an orderly way, too, with a sense of finality. We both agree that all books should have "The End" written on the last page.

Nobody came in the shop while we were talking, so we went into the back room for a few minutes to start unpacking some of the boxes that have started coming in as the result of Aunt Beverly's buying trip. What wonderful things she ordered! She had one entire box of tiny silver frames—just the right size for school pictures. Another box had tiny little pillows filled with potpourri. They smelled good enough to eat.

Lots of the boxes had candles, of all different sizes and shapes.

"Aunt Beverly!" I said teasingly. "Are you expecting a candlelight dinner any time soon?"

She sighed. "Not really. I haven't seen Mr. Wonderful Customer all week, and it doesn't look as if he's coming in this morning."

No sooner had she said those words than the string of bells on the shop door began to jingle, indicating that a customer had come in. I peeked around the corner and quickly said, "On the other hand . . ." Aunt Beverly was already on her feet and headed out of the stockroom to greet Mr. Clark Weaver.

This time I was determined to get a better look at him. I kept forgetting all week to ask Jon if he had a relative named Clark. I thought that maybe if I could see his face, I would see a resemblance. I tried to walk casually around the counter by the coffees, candies, and teas . . . only to find myself walking into a dead end. Aunt Beverly had some unopened boxes of coffee and candy stacked on the floor at the end of the counter. That meant . . . I was trapped behind the counter as Aunt Beverly and Mr. Clark Weaver came walking toward the cash register. How embarrassing.

Aunt Beverly didn't seem to mind my being there, though. She said casually, "This is my niece, Katelyn. She'll ring up your purchase for you." And with that, Aunt Beverly disappeared quickly into the back room.

I guess that was Aunt Beverly's way of acting at ease, as if she didn't care whether Mr. Clark Weaver was in the shop or not. I took the book from him and rang up the sale as I asked, "Do you need any coffee, candy, or tea?"

He said, "Actually, I would like a little more of that decaffeinated Swiss Almond coffee that Beverly recommended the last time I was in."

Beverly? I couldn't help but notice that he knew Aunt Beverly's name. Then again, she does wear a little gold name plate on her dress, and the business cards by the cash register also have her name on them. Still, he "sounded personal," as Gramma Weber would have said.

"How much would you like?" I asked as I moved toward the coffee tins. All the time, of course, I was trying to look at him carefully without being too obvious. I really couldn't see any resemblance to Jon. From what I could tell, Mr. Clark Weaver has blond curly hair and is quite a bit taller than Jon. He doesn't wear glasses, and he wasn't wearing a shirt with a button-down collar. He had on a T-shirt and shorts, sandals, an old golf cap, and sunglasses dangling around his neck on a leather cord. His voice didn't sound like Jon's, either.

"One pound will be fine," he said. I filled the sack and added it to the receipt, when all of a sudden, a zany thought hit me. "Would you like any candles? We just got in some particularly beautiful ones."

Mr. Clark Weaver grinned. And that gave him away. It was *exactly* the same grin I'd seen on Jon's face more times than I can count. *He is related,* I thought. *Now I just have to find out how!* "Well," I said, "you just might want to invite someone over sometime for a candlelight dinner."

"Oh?" he replied, with a little tease in his voice. *Yes . . . he definitely must be related. Jon almost always sounds like he's teasing a little.* "Any ideas about whom I might invite?"

"Oh, one or two," I said coyly, secretly hoping that Aunt Beverly wasn't listening. She'd have my head.

To my surprise, he said, "Well, let's see what kind of candles you have." I quickly reached for the box we had just put on the counter to sort and said, "Here are some that look like they'd go on a table at a man's house."

He reached over to pick up and examine a couple of the navy-blue tapers and said, "You just might have a good idea, Miss Katelyn. I'll take these two."

And there you have it. I just *know* there's a candlelight dinner in Aunt Beverly's future.

As I finished ringing up the sale and putting his purchases in a sack, Aunt Beverly returned to the shop . . . just in time to watch Mr. Clark Weaver walk toward the front door.

"Rats," she said. "I didn't even get much chance to talk to him this week."

"Where did you go?" I asked.

"Didn't you hear the phone ring?"

"No, I guess I was too nervous about waiting on Mr. Wonderful and trying to see if he looked like Jon Weaver."

"And does he?" Aunt Beverly asked.

"Not really," I said. "But he has *exactly* the same grin, and he likes to tease—which is just like Jon."

"Hmmm," Aunt Beverly responded. "I wonder if and how they might be related."

"Me, too." And with that, we both fell silent for a few minutes, unpacking more of the candles and putting them on a shelf at a slant so people could see all the different colors and styles. A few of the candles we put in some candle holders that were also a part of the week's shipment. I especially like the ones made out of pewter. They look like something straight out of *The House of the Seven Gables* by Nathaniel Hawthorne. A great book. Aunt Beverly carries it in her store as one of the classics.

Aunt Beverly broke the silence by asking, "Didn't you say that you had *two* exciting things to tell me?"

"Yes!" I said. "I can't believe I didn't tell you the second one! Kimber called me last night, and next Sunday—not tomorrow, but the day after we get back from graduation in Eagle Point—there's going to be a youth group swimming party! It's going to be at the home of one of the kids in the group and everyone's invited!"

"Who's Kimber?" Aunt Beverly asked.

"She's the girl who came in with Kiersten and Mari last week."

"I thought her name was Kim."

"It is—well, according to Kiersten. Actually, her name is Kimberly and her family calls her Kimmie, but her friends call her Kimber."

"Oh . . . and you two have become friends, I take it?"

"Yes! I can't believe I didn't tell you that. We went to church together last Sunday morning— Dad and Kiersten, too—and then Kimber and I went to the youth group last Sunday night. It was neat."

"I'm really glad to hear that," Aunt Beverly said. "I've been praying you'd make a friend . . . in addition to Jon Weaver, of course."

"Well, your prayers have been answered," I said. "Not only is Kimber a new friend, but I've got another new friend at school. Her name is Libby—short for Elizabeth." I told Aunt Beverly what had happened at school on Thursday, and by that time it was nearly noon. Aunt Beverly and I went into the back room to unwrap our sandwiches, and no sooner had we each taken a bite than customers began to flood into the store. We both were working nonstop for almost three hours! We sold almost half of the new little silver frames and lots of candles and potpourri pillows. Aunt Beverly made some good choices! Between customers, Aunt Beverly or I would go into the back and sneak a bite or two of our sandwiches. It was definitely an afternoon of lunch on the run. We didn't have a chance to talk again until late in the afternoon.

"Do you have a swimsuit for the party?" Aunt Beverly asked.

"I don't know if I can fit into last year's suit or not," I said.

"Well, we'd better close up the shop a half hour early, then, and run over to Clara's to see if we can find you one." Clara's is a dress shop in Collinsville, right up the street from The Wonderful Life Shop. It has clothes for women of all ages—from baby dresses to grandmother dresses. In fact, that's what the sign says just under the name "Clara's"—"A shop for women of all ages." When I was little, Mom took me there every time we came to Collinsville to visit Grandpa Stone.

So, to get back to my story, Aunt Beverly and I closed up the shop at four-thirty instead of the usual five o'clock, and we went to Clara's and I got the cutest swimsuit I've ever seen. It's navy—a one piece—with red piping around the halter top and the leg openings. It has small white anchors embroidered across the top of the suit. And not only that, but Aunt Beverly bought me a cute navy-and-white-stripe cover-up that's like a great big shirt, and also a fairly longish full red skirt. I can wear either the skirt or the shirt over the swimsuit—or both. Aunt Beverly has great fashion sense. I hope I take after her in that department, too.

Afterward, Aunt Beverly and I stopped at McGreggor's to get a soda. It's just down the hill from Clara's. McGreggor's is one of my favorite places in all of Collinsville, and probably all the world—except, of course, that I haven't yet seen all the world. It's a real old-fashioned drug store with a creaky wooden floor and high ceilings, and a soda fountain just like you see in the old-timey movies. There's one long counter that's just for cosmetics—all kinds of fun things and lots of different brands. Another long display shelf has nothing but greeting cards. Some of them look like they've been there for years, but that makes them seem even more special in my eyes. In the summer, the store has a big ceiling fan that keeps the air circulating. Dad says McGreggor's looks like a Norman Rockwell painting straight off the cover of *The Saturday Evening Post.* I agree—and I love it. McGreggor's smells like a combination of ice cream, medicines, and perfume. It's a great place to visit, and an especially great place to get a chocolate soda made with chocolate ice cream. That's what Aunt Beverly and I always order.

While we were sipping our sodas, and Aunt Beverly was worrying (at least pretending to worry a little bit) about spoiling my appetite for dinner . . . she said, "I have some news to tell you, too, Katelyn. We've been so busy today that I haven't thought to tell you until now."

"What is it?" I couldn't tell from the sound of her voice whether this was going to be good news or bad news. "Is it good news?"

"Yes, I think it is . . . mostly," she said. "You know Mrs. Miller, don't you—the woman who comes to clean my house once a week and who also cleans Grandpa's house and helps him with his ironing?"

"Sure, I know Mrs. Miller," I said. "She's the

one who makes casseroles for Grandpa, too, isn't she?"

"Well, yes," said Aunt Beverly. "I hadn't thought about that, but yes, she has been making casseroles for Grandpa while she's there at his house cleaning and ironing."

"They're good," I said. "Grandpa had us over to dinner a couple of times while you were on your buying trip."

"Great," said Aunt Beverly. "Then you know that Mrs. Miller can cook. That's part of what I'm about to tell you." After another sip of her soda, Aunt Beverly continued. "Your grandpa and dad and I got together a couple of days ago for lunch and we made a decision that we hope is going to work for all of us. We've hired Mrs. Miller full-time to be our cook and housekeeper. She agreed to the job just yesterday, and she'll start next week."

"Does that mean you'll be coming over every night for supper?" I asked. Ever since we moved to Collinsville, Aunt Beverly has been at our house for supper every few nights or so, except of course for the time that she went on her buying trip. She and Dad would combine their efforts to come up with something for dinner, and Kiersten and I usually helped in some way. Well, actually, the most Kiersten can do is set the table and help clear up afterward, but I've been helping make the salads.

It's been fun having everybody gather in the kitchen and pitch in to fix dinner and then eat it together. Sometimes Grandpa Stone has joined us, too. On nights when Aunt Beverly doesn't come over, Dad and I just make sandwiches and soup, or we go out for pizza at Tony's, which is a couple of stores down from Stone's Hardware. Come to think of it, we had a lot of pizza last week.

"Well, it probably means that I'll be there most nights—and so will Grandpa—but this is how I think this is going to work. Mrs. Miller is going to clean Grandpa's house and do his laundry and ironing on Tuesday and Thursday mornings. She'll clean my house and help me with some chores on Monday and Wednesday mornings. And then she'll be at your house on Friday mornings and every afternoon—Monday through Friday. At your house, she's not only going to help with the cleaning and laundry, but she's going to fix the evening meal for all of us. And Grandpa, your dad, Kiersten, you, and I will all have dinner together on most nights. How does that sound?"

"It sounds wonderful!" I said.

Aunt Beverly sighed as she finished her soda. "I think it's going to mean a little easier workload for all of us." I don't think I realized until that moment that our coming to Collinsville may have meant more work for Aunt Beverly. Suddenly, I was very glad to know that Mrs. Miller was going to be helping us.

"That's not all," Aunt Beverly said. "Mrs. Miller has a granddaughter who is coming to stay with her this summer. Her name is Trish and she's just your age."

"Really?" I said. "That will be one more friend!"

"I hope it works out that way," said Aunt Beverly. "I know you've already made a couple of friends and that not everybody you meet will turn out to *be* a friend, but I'm hoping that you can be friends with Trish. This is probably going to be a difficult summer for her."

"What's wrong?" I asked. "Is there something you aren't telling me?"

"Well, Katie," Aunt Beverly said, "I'm not sure just how much I *should* tell you. Trish's mom and dad are going through a rough time right now in their marriage and the main reason that Trish is coming to visit her grandmother is so they can try to come to a decision about whether they should stay married or get a divorce. Trish really doesn't want to come to Collinsville. Mrs. Miller said that she thinks if she comes, her parents will get a divorce for sure, but that if she stays with them in Fruitvale, they will stay married. So she's not really all that excited about being here, and Mrs. Miller is afraid that she may even try to run away."

"Oh," I said. That was a lot to think about!

"There. I've told you the whole thing and I wasn't even sure I should tell you any of it. I don't know what kind of girl Trish is, and I probably shouldn't have told you any of this so that you could just meet her and get to know her without any preconceptions. Still, I think maybe you can have a good influence on Trish."

"When is she coming?"

"Mrs. Miller says that her school is out next Friday, so she'll be ready to come to Collinsville on Saturday, the same day we're returning from Eagle Point. Mrs. Miller called the shop this morning—in fact, that was the call that kept me from talking to Mr. Clark Weaver—and she said she had talked to your dad and the plan is for us to pick up Trish in Fruitvale on our way back from your graduation."

"Sounds good to me," I said. "And don't worry, Aunt Beverly. I'm not worried about whether I'll like Trish or not. All I can do is be friendly to her and if we become friends, we become friends. If we don't, we don't. If she has problems, maybe I can help her with them. We'll just have to see."

"That's my girl," said Aunt Beverly. And of course, I got a hug.

"Maybe Trish would like to go to the swim party next Sunday with Kimber and me."

"You think that would be OK?"

"Well, Kimber said that everybody was invited

and that Bert and Sharyn had talked to the parents who are giving the party, and they said that we should invite friends who might be interested in becoming a part of Faith Community Fellowship. I'm inviting Libby to go, too."

"I guess maybe I'd better call Mrs. Miller so she can make sure that Trish brings her swimsuit."

And that, Journal, is how Saturday went. I've got a lot going all of a sudden, don't I? Dad would call them "upcoming attractions." There's gradua-tion . . . and the swim party . . . and a possible new friend named Trish. It's going to be an inter-esting week ahead!

Chapter Six

Clearing the Air

*I*t was *déjà vu*—well, sorta. I just learned that phrase and so I just had to use it. I was sitting in Emily's Place today enjoying lunch—really, for the first time in several days. Last Friday and yesterday I had lunch with Libby in the patio cafeteria, but today, her mom picked her up to have her run an errand with her over the lunch hour, so I grabbed a sandwich and headed for Emily's Place. It kinda felt like coming home—back to a familiar place. I can't help but wonder what it will be like to go to Eagle Point this weekend. It seems like a long time ago, now, that we lived there.

Anyway . . . as I was sitting there I looked up to see Jon Weaver standing in the archway that connects the little courtyard to the park—just like he was standing there almost two weeks ago.

"We've got to talk," he said.

There was something about his tone of voice that I didn't particularly like.

"OK," I said, putting down my book. "What is it?"

"It's about your mom," he said.

"What about Mom?" I asked. I was really surprised that he would bring her up. We've never talked about her before.

"Well, we're friends, aren't we, Katelyn?" Jon said.

"I hope so. I like to think we are," I replied.

"I feel the same way," he said, and there was that old familiar grin. "And I just can't imagine your mom dating my dad. It's weird. And you also said that your dad is in Collinsville—working with your grandpa at Stone's Hardware. So I also can't figure out why your mom is being so friendly with my dad." Jon stopped to take a deep breath before he continued, "I guess you could say I'm sorta confused, and confusion is *not* what a computer nerd should be noted for. Care to help me out?"

"In the first place, you're not a nerd," I said. "I wish you would quit calling yourself that. My friends *aren't* nerds."

"Yes, ma'am," said Jon, straightening and giving me a mock salute. "But until you come up with a better name than weevil . . . I'm kinda stuck in that mode." I was glad to see his grin return.

"In the second place, you can't possibly be talking about my mother. My mother died last year in an automobile accident."

"Oh, wow, I'm sorry," Jon said. "I really put my foot in it. I had no idea . . ."

"It's OK. We can talk about it sometime, but it's still pretty painful for me to tell people I don't know very well."

"So who is Beverly Weber?"

Aha! The lights were starting to come on.

"Beverly Weber is my aunt!"

"Your aunt?"

"Yes. She owns The Wonderful Life Shop. And your father must be Mr. Clark Weaver."

"That's right," Jon said. "What a relief. I was having visions that you could end up being my stepsister." He pretended to groan, but it's hard to groan when you are grinning.

"Is that such a terrible idea?"

"Not really. I just like you better as a friend."

My brain was spinning. What Jon was telling me was that his father was interested in Aunt Beverly! But what about Jon's mother?

"I'm almost afraid to ask," I said, "but what about your mother. Is she alive?"

"No, she died when I was just two years old. I

really don't remember anything about her. It's been just Dad and me all these years."

"You never have told me how you came to live in Collinsville," I said.

"Well, you never asked," said Jon. "And for that matter, I don't know how *you* happened to move here, either."

"So who goes first?" I asked.

"You first," he said. So I told Jon about what Grandpa had said about the hardware store, and about Aunt Beverly living here, and how we decided it was the best thing for all of us to be together as a family in one town. And then Jon told me a little about his dad and how they happened to move here.

We must have talked for twenty minutes, because we nearly missed hearing the bell and had to race across the park to get to class. Fortunately, my history teacher was a little late so I didn't get docked for being tardy.

I'll try to put down for you, Journal, as much as I can remember about what Jon said, but I'm sure I'm going to leave something out.

Jon's mother died trying to give birth to what would have been Jon's baby sister. The baby girl died, too. It was a strange accident in the hospital that caused their deaths, but because the doctor was partly at fault, Jon's father received a settlement of money that gave him the freedom to travel a little. Which is what he decided to do. Jon said that some of his first memories are of being carried in a backpack of sorts on his dad's back.

Jon and his dad roamed around the country and even went to several other countries before his dad finally decided that he needed to settle down and get Jon into school. Jon said that he thinks his father kept moving around because he missed his mother so much. By the time they settled down in Oak Hills—which is about fifty miles from Collinsville—Jon was eight. His dad had taught him to read and write and spell and do math while they were traveling, so Jon didn't start school without knowing anything. In fact, he was ahead of his classmates in lots of areas, so the teachers let him play with a computer to occupy his time while the other students learned some of the basic things that Jon already knew. That's how Jon got to be so good at computers. He's been using them since he was eight! He can't believe that I'd never even touched one until we did the aptitude test in Miss Kattenhorn's office.

Jon's dad is a real athlete. They moved to Collinsville when he was offered the position of being the manager and part owner of the new Collinsville Family Fitness Center. He also advises a lot of executives in Benton—that's the major city that's about thirty-five miles from here—about what kinds of exercise equipment they should buy, and how they should set up exercise labs in their companies. He's into sailing and golf and all kinds of sports.

And no, Journal, he's never remarried. Jon said that Aunt Beverly is the first person that he's ever really seemed to be very interested in or has even mentioned. Jon said he was shocked when his dad told him that he'd met someone at a bookshop that he might like to date—and that he was even more shocked when he told Jon that the woman's name was Beverly Weber.

"I was shocked when I found out that there was a Mr. Clark Weaver!" I said to Jon. "I tried to figure out if you were related, but you really don't look much like your dad."

"No. All the relatives say I look more like my mother."

"Except," I said, "you have his grin."

"Yeah, I guess I do," said Jon. And of course, he grinned.

I could hardly wait to tell Aunt Beverly all of this, of course, but wouldn't you know—she left a note on the kitchen counter saying that she had gone to Benton to meet some friends for dinner, so I won't be able to see her until tomorrow. I'm not sure I can wait that long!

That isn't all that happened today, though. All in all, it was a pretty big day for having major talks.

Libby came back from lunch pretty depressed. She said that her mother had taken her to see a speech therapist and that she was going to have to start making regular visits to see a Dr. Thompson—maybe as many as three times a week.

"Why do you dread going?" I asked her.

"B-b-b-because," she said, "these therapists are nearly always alike. This one has a Ph.D., so she'll probably be even worse than some of the others. They all try to figure out what it was that caused me to s-s-s-start stuttering. I've had trouble ever since I can remember. I w-w-w-wish they would just work on how I can get over it. I don't need a c-c-c-counselor as much as I need to know how to quit."

"I see your point." And then I felt I had to add, "But who knows? Maybe this speech therapist will be different. My sister, Kiersten, went to a speech therapist back in Eagle Point and he really helped her."

"Did she s-s-s-stutter?" Libby asked.

"No. But she couldn't make the sound of an 'r' until she was nearly eight years old. For lots of years, Dad and Mom and I were the only ones who could really understand her. The therapist helped her a lot. In fact, sometimes I think he helped her too much. She can't stop talking now!"

Libby laughed and I was glad to see that I had helped her feel a little better.

"Hey, I've been meaning to ask you for two days," I said. "Do you want to go to a swim party with me next Sunday night? It's being held as part of our youth group meeting—the youth group at Faith Community Fellowship. Lots of kids will be there and it would be a good chance for you to make some friends."

"Well . . . I don't know," said Libby.

"Don't know what?" I asked.

"In the first place, I'm not a great swimmer."

"That's all right. Lots of people aren't. The only reason I really know how to swim well is because I grew up in Eagle Point, which is right on Eagle Bay. You kinda have to know how to swim in Eagle Point because it's just about the only thing there is to do in the summers. If you want, I can help you learn to swim this summer. I've already promised to help teach Mari, my little sister's friend."

"Thanks. I think I'd really like that," said Libby, "but . . ."

"But what?" I knew I was hounding Libby but that's part of my nature, I guess. Besides, I really wanted her to go to the party.

"I don't look all that g-g-g-great in a swimsuit."

"Good grief," I said. "Nobody will care about that."

"I c-c-c-care," said Libby.

"We all think we look stupid in our swimsuits," I said.

"But you're not fat," said Libby.

"You aren't either!" I protested.

"Yes, I am. I should lose at least ten pounds," said Libby.

"Who says?" I asked. "Did a doctor tell you that?"

"Well, no," admitted Libby. "A doctor didn't have to tell me. I can tell it myself."

"I think you look just fine," I said.

Libby looked at me as if I was stupid . . . but friendly stupid. She said, "I was b-b-b-born five pounds overweight and I've been overweight all my life. It's almost worse than stuttering."

"How can you be born five pounds over-weight?" I asked, trying to tease her out of her mood.

"I really was!" she said. "I weighed eleven pounds when I was born and a normal baby in our family weighs six pounds! That's five pounds overweight."

I laughed. "Libby Webster, you *are* going to the party with me on Sunday night. If you sit on the side of the pool wearing a cover-up all night, that's fine with me. But you *are* going."

"Oh?" she said. I could tell, though, that she had just about decided to go.

"Oh," I said. "The party begins at seven o'clock, so you'd better be ready when Dad and I stop by to pick you up."

So much for conversation number two.

The most difficult conversation just happened a little while ago and I'm still not sure what to think or what I should do next.

Kiersten came into my room right after supper, and with big tears in her eyes, she said, "I'm homesick."

I could hardly believe I was hearing this from Kiersten. Kiersten—my bubbly, giggly, cute little sister who bounces everywhere and in Grandpa Stone's words, has "a sunshine personality." Kiersten . . . the one who is always quick to make friends. Whatever could she mean?

"Want to talk about it?" I asked. I couldn't think of anything else to say.

"I miss the way things were. Mom and Dad and the house in Eagle Point."

"I do, too, Kiersti," I said. "Sometimes I wish we could turn back the clock a couple of years and have everything be just the way it was."

"You do?" she said, sounding surprised.

"Sure, I do. There isn't a day that goes by that I don't miss Mom and think about all the good times we had together as a family in Eagle Point."

"Oh," she said. "I thought you liked it here."

"I do," I said. "At least I'm liking it more every day. It helps to be making some friends. But liking it here doesn't mean that I don't miss the way things were."

"It doesn't?"

"No. You can like one place and still miss the other place, too."

"I thought maybe something was wrong with me," said Kiersten, wiping her eyes. "Everybody seems to like it here so much and nobody ever talks about Eagle Point or even mentions Mom."

I thought back over the past several weeks since the move and realized that Kiersten was right, to an extent. We hadn't mentioned Mom very much—at least not as often as we had in Eagle Point.

"Just because we don't talk about Mom all the time doesn't mean that we don't think about her, Kiersti. I think about Mom all the time."

"I'm afraid I'm going to forget what she was like," said Kiersten.

"Oh, you won't forget," I said. I held out my arms toward her and invited her to come sit in my lap as I sat in the big old yellow chair in my bedroom. She came over and let me cuddle her and hold her almost like a baby.

"How can you be so sure?"

"Well, in the first place, Dad and Aunt Beverly and I won't let you forget. And in the second place, you're a lot like Mom. There's a big part of Mom in *you*. Sometimes you say and do things and I find myself thinking, *That's just what Mom would have said* or, *That's just what Mom used to do.* Even if you think you're forgetting, you aren't."

"Are you scared to go back to Eagle Point this weekend?"

"Scared? No. I'm really looking forward to it. This is my graduation from junior high. Do you know how many years I looked forward to graduating and being in high school?—and now I am. It's what Gramma Weber would call a 'milestone.' Are you scared?"

"A little."

"Do you know what you're scared about?" I asked.

"Well, I'm scared that my friends might not remember me . . . and that I might cry when we walk into the old house . . . and that I might not remember my way around Eagle Point."

"I'll make you a deal," I said. "I'll help you find your way around town, and if your friends don't remember you, I'll introduce them to you!" I tickled her a little. And then I got an idea. "Get up."

Kiersten scrambled to get out of the chair as I got up and went to my dresser. I pulled open a drawer and handed her a handkerchief with a big pink "E" embroidered on one corner. "And if you cry, well, here's one of Mom's handkerchiefs to wipe your tears away."

"Oh, Katelyn," Kiersten said, as she came over

and threw her arms around my waist. "I'm glad you're my sister."

"Ninety percent of the time, I am, too," I said. "Now, get out of here before the other ten percent kicks in."

I hope I helped Kiersten. Maybe I shouldn't have sent her back to her room so soon. I'll see how she feels tomorrow. For now, the best thing I can probably do is say an extra prayer for her tonight before I go to sleep.

I have a big day ahead of me. Aunt Beverly and I are going shopping for graduation dresses, and we may go all the way over to Benton if Clara's doesn't have the right dress.

Chapter Seven

A New Look

Thursday
9 P.M.

I hardly know where to begin. In the last twenty-four hours I feel as if my life has changed completely. Well, at least the way I look.

It all started when Aunt Beverly and I went shopping for a graduation dress. Aunt Beverly got Mrs. Campbell—a neighbor woman who used to work at McGreggor's—to watch the shop for her so she could pick me up at three o'clock, right when I got out of school. We immediately went to Clara's to see what they had. I liked a couple of the dresses—one was pale blue with a big satin waistband, the other a pink eyelet dress, but Aunt Beverly whispered to me that she didn't think either of them was special enough. So, after quick calls to Dad and to Mrs. Miller to tell them we

81

wouldn't be home for dinner, we were off to Benton in search of "the dress."

We went first to Norton's, a big department store at the Benton South Mall. I've been there once before and it truly is an amazing store. There certainly isn't anything like it in Collinsville, much less Eagle Point. We didn't see anything there that was any prettier than the dresses at Clara's, though. Aunt Beverly didn't even see anything she wanted me to try on. This is the first time I've ever seen Aunt Beverly so determined to find "just the right thing." I can't help but wonder if she's like that on her buying trips. If she is, it explains why she brings home so many wonderful things.

Anyway . . . after a look in a couple of other stores there at the mall, Aunt Beverly said, "I don't know why I haven't thought of this before. We're going to have to hurry to make sure they're still open, but I think I know just the place for us to look!" And we were off.

We ended up at a place called Marlena's Shoppe. It was about ten minutes away from the mall, in a residential part of Benton. In fact, it didn't look like a shop at all—more like a house, although it did have big picture windows with mannequins in them, wearing very stylish clothes.

When we walked in, I knew immediately that

this wasn't like any other dress shop I had ever been in. In the first place, there were no racks of clothes, only two or three more mannequins in various parts of the room, and several groupings of sofas and chairs. The room was carpeted in a very thick gold carpet and a big crystal chandelier hung from the center of the room. I said to Aunt Beverly, "This feels very expensive." Aunt Beverly just smiled.

Within seconds after we had walked in, a woman came out of one of the side doors and asked us how she could help us. Aunt Beverly said, "We're looking for a very elegant, but still youthful dress—tea length—for my niece's graduation from junior high school. Nothing too frilly or sweet, but nothing too after five-ish."

I'm not sure what all that meant, but the woman nodded and disappeared. Aunt Beverly and I sat on one of the love seats and watched a woman across the room being shown some suits by another of the sales ladies. Within a few minutes, the woman who was helping us reappeared with several dresses draped over her arms. She hung them on a brass rod and began showing them to us one by one. Aunt Beverly pointed out things she liked or didn't like about each dress, and the woman again nodded. This time she smiled and said, "I think I have just the dress for you." She disappeared again behind a side door and a couple of minutes later reappeared. She was holding the most beautiful dress I have ever seen in my life. I could hardly wait to try it on.

The woman ushered Aunt Beverly and me to a very large dressing room just off the main area where we had been sitting. It was nearly the size of my bedroom at home and had full-length mirrors on three sides of the room. Aunt Beverly helped me into the dress and we both knew immediately that this was *the* dress for me!

It had a lace-like top, with tiny seed pearls and a few clear sequins scattered here and there. The top had cap sleeves and was "form fitting" as Gramma Weber would say. The skirt was full—several thicknesses of chiffon—and it hit the middle of my calves. Aunt Beverly called it "tea length." At the waist was a narrow satin belt that tied in the back. The front of the dress had a "boat" neckline—sorta straight across from shoulder to shoulder, but the back of the dress was more bare—the neckline scooped down to just above my bra. The entire dress was a light creamy beige. The sales lady called it "champagne."

I have never felt so elegant in all my life as I did when I put on that dress. Aunt Beverly smiled and said very simply, "At last. Something truly special for my very special niece." It was my turn to give *her* a hug at that point! I can hardly wait to get to Eagle Point now.

After we had supper at Mexico Pete's, we went shoe shopping and Aunt Beverly decided that I should have cloth shoes dyed the same color as the dress. We found a shop that could dye shoes overnight so we told them we'd come back the next afternoon.

Over supper, Aunt Beverly asked me if I had ever thought about changing my hairstyle. I could see the wheels turning in her head. "Actually, I've never given it much thought," I said. "I'm not sure what else I might be able to do with my hair, except to pull it back with a headband or french braid it. It's so wavy, you know."

"Well," said Aunt Beverly, "I think you might want to try a new look, especially since you're leaving junior high in such a dramatic dress."

"I'm game," I said. "What do you think?"

"How about more curls?" she said. "And maybe a few blond highlights."

"You mean a permanent?" I said with a shudder. "I've never had much luck with permanents, Aunt Beverly. You remember that time I ended up looking like frizz city?"

"Yes, I do," said Aunt Beverly with a grimace. "That's *not* what I had in mind. I think the guy I go to for my permanents might be just the ticket. If you're up for it, I'll see if I can get an appointment tomorrow after school—we have to come back over to Benton to get your shoes anyway."

"All right," I said. I tried to sound cheerful about it, but frankly, Journal, I was really nervous about that permanent. We had just purchased the most beautiful dress I've ever seen and I didn't want to see anything detract from it—*especially* frizzy hair.

That isn't the way it turned out, though. Mr. Ray—the man who does Aunt Beverly's hair—was really neat. He suggested that the highlights come later because he didn't want my hair to get too dry or brittle. We talked about different styles a little bit. And then he went to work. I've never seen anybody roll a permanent as fast as he did. He cut my hair a couple of inches and gave me some wispy bangs and by the time he was finished . . . well, let's put it this way—I hardly recognized the girl in the mirror!

I had soft big curls framing my face—about halfway to my shoulders. My hair seemed fuller than ever before. Mr. Ray said, "It's all in the cut." Best of all . . . no frizz. And no waves. Just wonderful curls.

"Is that me, Aunt Beverly?" I asked as a joke as Mr. Ray twirled me around in the chair so I could see the back of my head in the mirror.

"I'm not sure this was such a good idea," she said.

"You don't like it?" I asked. "I love it!"

"I like it just fine. I'm just not sure that I did the

right thing helping you to turn into such a beauty. You look so much older and more sophisticated!"

"Like a novelist?" I asked, teasing her.

"Like a world-famous best-selling novelist," she said.

While we were at Mr. Ray's salon, Aunt Beverly had a woman give me a manicure while I was waiting for the perm to "cook," as Mr. Ray said. That was the first manicure I've ever had in a salon. My nails have never looked better. The nail stylist put on fake nails and then colored them with a pale pink polish. I'm trying to be very careful with them.

But, Journal, that still isn't all. When we went back to the mall to pick up my shoes, we stopped by one of the cosmetic counters at Norton's. Aunt Beverly asked one of the women there if they could help us with some makeup.

I've never really worn much makeup. I've always been blessed with a pretty good complexion. Just a few months ago I started wearing a little mascara and a little lipstick.

This woman helped me find a very light water-based makeup and she also taught me how to put on just a hint of eye shadow and blush. I must admit, a little color does wonders.

"Is all this really happening to me?" I asked Aunt Beverly as we left Norton's. "I feel like Cinderella, being transformed to go to the ball."

"Well, I'm *not* a fairy godmother," Aunt Beverly laughed.

"No?" I said. "If you're not, you're the next best thing."

And there you have it . . . the new me!

Dad was in shock, as you might imagine. I saw Aunt Beverly and Dad talking over in a corner of the kitchen, and I could tell Dad was a little upset. I couldn't hear much of what they said, just a few phrases from Aunt Beverly, such as "she's not a little girl anymore, Fred" . . . "this is a special weekend for her" . . . and "she's still the same sweet girl on the inside."

I hope I am. Something inside me feels a lot older all of a sudden.

Kiersten, of course, was beside herself. She was bouncing all over the house and had to call Mari to come over right away to see her "new sister." Kimber came over, too, and she really liked the new look. I was glad she approved. "You're a knockout," she said. "I'm going to have to see if your Aunt Beverly can help me!" Actually, Kimber doesn't need any help. She's beautiful right now.

It seems like forever until we leave for Eagle Point, but in reality, I know it's less than twelve hours. In a way, I wish I could go to school tomorrow before we leave. I'd like for Libby to see the new me . . . and also Jon Weaver. I wonder if he'll like what he sees.

Chapter Eight

Return
to
Eagle Point

I have no doubt that I could find my way around Eagle Point with a blindfold on. In the first place, it's the only place I ever lived before we moved to Collinsville, which means that I lived there for fourteen and a half years. In the second place, Eagle Point isn't all that big. The population sign now says 4,845. Actually, it has said that for a couple of years. In the third place, Eagle Point is laid out in a very straightforward way—like terraces up the side of a hill. There's really only one main street in town—it just winds its way back and forth parallel to the water. Occasional cross streets cut through at angles, but there aren't very many of those.

Eagle Point is located on Eagle Bay. Behind the top row of houses is the bluff. The bluff gets the

89

best of the breezes and there's a great view of the bay from there. On top of the bluff is an old saw-mill that's no longer in use. There's forest to the north and south of Eagle Point, and most of the lumber now goes to Castle Rock, a few miles up the coastline. People get to Eagle Point on a road that leads through a canyon that's just to the north of the bluff.

The main industry in Eagle Point is tourism. In the summers, the town is filled with people who rent the houses right next to the bay, or who stay in one of the seven small bed-and-breakfast inns close to the water. That's where the cafés and two or three art galleries are also located. Mom used to hang her paintings at one of the galleries and several of them sold every summer to the tour-ists. In fact, the galleries are one of the main rea-sons that Mom and Dad chose to live in Eagle Point. Summer is the busiest time, but Eagle Point seems to have lots of visitors year-round, mostly on weekends. Dad says that at least one in every four houses is a "weekend" house, and when Dad worked as a contractor, weekend houses were mostly what he built.

The beach at Eagle Point is small, but clean. There's really not much to do if you're a kid in Eagle Point except go to the beach, glide down the main street on your bicycle (if traffic isn't too heavy), and sit and watch the tourists come and go. There's a pier and a small marina that jut out into the bay. Some of the tourists come mainly to go sailing. Kiersten and I both learned to sail when we were really young. In fact, I don't remember a time when I couldn't sail. We have a little catamaran that we've named the *K. K. Kruiser.* *K. K.* stands for Katelyn and Kiersten, of course.

All in all, Eagle Point is a quiet place—a good place for relaxing, and as Mom used to say, "It's a good place to raise kids."

Kiersten and I loved living in Eagle Point. It never occurred to us that we might ever live anyplace else. We shared a blue-and-white bedroom with white frilly curtains at a big window that looked out over the bay. Mom used to say, "It's a small room but it has a big view." Nearly all the houses in Eagle Point are small, and the yards are even smaller. Most people just have decks or patios, no grass—our deck was bigger than average, and Mom had lots of big clay pots on it that she called her "garden." Some were planted with flowers, some with herbs, and two of the planters had miniature evergreen trees, which we decorated each Christmas. A giant ruby-red rhododendron plant covered a big part of the front half of the house.

It was good to be back in the house again after two months of being away. In some ways, it felt as if we were coming home from a vacation, although we have never taken a vacation that long. On the other hand, the house seemed different—probably because it had a lot less furniture in it. (We only left some of the bare essentials—beds, a few chairs, a sofa.) That, and the fact that things were pretty dusty and there weren't any flowers inside the house. When Mom was alive, she kept nearly every vase in the house filled with flowers. Kiersten and I continued to pick flowers after she died. It seemed like something Mom would have wanted us to do. Even though we were only going to be in Eagle Point overnight, Kiersten and I went out and picked some flowers for just that reason.

Dad said he's decided to keep the house for a while as a getaway place for us to use on weekends. I asked him if that meant we were going to become tourists and he just laughed and said, "Yes, but not the run-of-the-mill kind. We at least know our way around town." That's for sure.

We got to Eagle Point about noon—it's only about a three-hour drive from Collinsville. I didn't have to be at the rehearsal until 2:30, so Kiersten and I immediately set out to roam around town. We just followed our noses—turning whichever way we wanted each time we got to an intersection. We knew that we could always get home within a half hour. That's what we used to say to Mom. Give us half an hour, and we can get home from anywhere in Eagle Point!

All our friends, of course, were in school, so we didn't have as much fun as we might have had. Still, it was good to see lots of familiar sights and to smell the musty, wet smell of the bay air. It seemed a little strange not to have Scooter by our side as we wandered up and down the hills of the town. Dad had insisted that we leave him in Collinsville, in spite of Kiersten's protests.

Dad drove me to the school at 2:30 sharp, and it was a blast to see all my friends again. They loved my new look, and as you might imagine, they asked lots and lots and *lots* of questions about Collinsville and what high school was like and whether I'd made any new friends. I told them about Kimber and Libby, but for some reason, I wasn't all that comfortable telling them about Jon. I *know* my Eagle Point friends. They wouldn't believe he's just a *friend*. I noticed that some of the boys—Tom Samuels and Jimmy Henderson in particular—could hardly quit staring at me. That was fun.

The rehearsal went well. The band managed to make it through "Pomp and Circumstance" a dozen or so times as we practiced walking in and out and across the stage. The choir rehearsed its song, "I Believe." There are only thirty-six of us graduating, which is still a pretty big number considering the size of the town. I guess I should tell you that the students from Castle Rock come over to Eagle Point for junior high, and then the high school students from Eagle Point go to Castle Rock. The two towns are only about five miles apart so it works out pretty well.

After rehearsal, I came home to get dressed. Aunt Beverly helped me with my hair and makeup. Right before we left, Kiersten whispered in my ear, "You look like a princess." She can be a real sweetheart at times. We had dinner at the Harbor House restaurant, where we saw several other families of graduates who had apparently decided to add to the celebration by eating out. (Aunt Beverly had said there really was no reason for us to stock up on groceries and cook at the house since we were only going to be there overnight. I was glad. I've always liked Harbor House and it made the night seem like more of a party.)

While we were at dinner, Dad, Aunt Beverly, and Kiersten handed me three boxes. I hadn't even thought about graduation presents! I opened Kiersten's present first and inside I found a beautiful clothbound blank book—my next book to write in as a journal!

The gift from Dad almost made me cry. He gave me a necklace that had been Mom's—three small pearls on a real gold chain. It was a necklace that Mom wore a lot and I feel really proud to have it now. I don't think I'll ever take it off. Also in the box were two small pearl earrings. I put the necklace and earrings on right away, of course. I hadn't thought I could feel any more elegant, but once I had on Mom's necklace and my new earrings, I felt even *more special*.

Aunt Beverly gave me a silver frame, which she said I was to use for a picture of myself in my graduation dress. My dress and shoes and perm were her major gift to me and I was really surprised that she had added anything else. "It's for a memory," she said on the card that she had taped to the frame. Just like Aunt Beverly!

The graduation ceremony started right on schedule, and for the most part, things went without a hitch. The microphone squawked a time or two, and poor Mitch Klausen tripped and nearly fell *up* the stairs of the platform, but nobody laughed and nobody really seemed to mind the technical trouble.

Bobby Somers got the award for Best Science Student, and Linda McGill got the award for Best All-Around Student. I thought I would be nervous going up to receive the Best English Student award, but when the time came, I wasn't nervous at all. Sandy Pierson won the competition to give the speech and she did a really good job. Tim Patterson, the student body president, offered the invocation.

Mr. Shell, our principal, read our names and handed us our diplomas, one by one. It just wouldn't be graduation without Mr. Shell reading the names in his big booming voice, adjusting his glasses between each name.

It was fun to hear everybody's formal first name and middle name. In my case, of course, there were two middle names to read. You rarely hear a person's full name. Some of them were a big surprise. It was all that Sarah Lindley—my best friend in Eagle Point—and I could do to keep from laughing when Mr. Shell announced Tommy Samuels as Thompson Horance Edgar Samuels. All these years we thought his first name was Thomas! We had no idea about the Horance or Edgar!

All in all, it was a great ceremony and I don't want to sound too proud, but I really did have the most beautiful dress. All the other girls said so, too.

After the ceremony, we met in the school cafeteria for a reception with the parents and other relatives of the graduates, and also friends from Eagle Point and Castle Rock who had come to see us graduate and wish us well. I was glad that Aunt Beverly had come, but felt a little sad that Grandpa Stone and Gramma Weber couldn't be there. Grandpa Stone caught a bad cold last week and Gramma Weber, of course, lives about seven hours away from Eagle Point. It was just too long a drive for her to make by herself. It was good to see my friends' parents again.

During the reception, an area was set aside for photographs. For just fifteen dollars, a graduate could have his or her photograph taken by a professional photographer in front of one of two settings—an archway that was just like the one we had walked through as we entered the patio area for the graduation ceremony, or a blown-up picture of the big gazebo that's at the back of the school, on a little hill overlooking the bay. I had a tough time deciding but finally chose the gazebo. It will remind me of Eagle Point. The photographer took three poses. In addition to that, Dad and Aunt Beverly both took lots of photos. I hope at least one of them turns out!

And then there was a party for just the graduates. It was held in the old gym and we had a good time playing games, drinking punch, eating cookies, and catching up on all the news. As the night wore on, I realized that not a whole lot had happened at Eagle Point since I left. In a strange way, that was comforting. I don't like to think of things changing in Eagle Point. Collinsville is enough change for me right now, thank you very much.

The biggest news was that the Pattersons have decided to move to Benton this summer. Everybody will really miss Tim. He's such a great guy.

I think if I had ever decided to have a boyfriend, I probably would have liked for him to have been Tim. I never heard Tim say anything bad about anybody, and besides that, he has a great sense of humor. In some ways, he reminds me of Jon Weaver.

The party ended at 11:30. When Aunt Beverly came to pick me up, I wasn't tired at all, but about half-way home, I found that I could hardly keep my eyes open. I was asleep the minute my head hit the pillow.

We were up pretty early the next morning and didn't even stop for breakfast in Eagle Point. We waited until we got to the crossroads, which is actually named Coren Ranch. Everybody, however, just calls it the crossroads because it's the place where Highway 42 and Pinkerton Road intersect. There's a big pancake house there that's been there for years, plus eight or nine houses, two gas stations, a burger stand, and the offices of a cattle ranch. Kiersten loves the waffles at the Crossroads Waffle House—I think it's because the waffles are in the shape of hearts. Stopping there was a real treat for her.

At the crossroads, we turned on Highway 42 instead of going on Pinkerton Road to Highway 139, which is the direct way back to Collinsville. Highway 42 winds through Fruitvale and eventually connects with Highway 139, and Fruitvale is where we were to pick up Trish Martin, Mrs. Miller's granddaughter.

We found her house very easily, from the directions that Mrs. Miller gave us, and Trish was packed and ready to go when we got there. I could tell she was sad—not at all eager to leave. She said hardly a word for the first several miles, even though Kiersten must have asked her a thousand questions. She really hit a streak, even for Kiersten.

Trish's graduation had been on Wednesday night, so after Kiersten gave up and decided to count cows out her window, Trish and I compared notes about our graduation ceremonies. Same song, of course. The whole world must use "Pomp and Circumstance." Trish seemed impressed that I was given the Best English Student award. Her school didn't give awards like that, but she told me that she really likes to read. That, of course, was the real ice breaker between us. We talked about books all the way back to Collinsville. We've got a number of favorites in common, and she also told me about a few books that I'd really like to see if I can find the next time I go to the library.

I noticed at one point that Aunt Beverly was smiling as she listened to Trish and me talk. I think she was feeling relieved that we found it easy to talk to each other, especially after all she had told me about Trish and her family. From what I can tell, Trish and I are going to have no problems being friends. She seems a bit opinionated at times, but I know I am, too. I can tell she has a good sense of humor, and that's a great trait, in my opinion.

The only time Trish got really quiet was when I invited her to the swim party tomorrow night. She said she'd have to think about that. I told her that she didn't need to go swimming if she didn't want to—I guess I'm a little sensitive about that after my talk with Libby—but that didn't seem to be the problem. She seemed more concerned that it was a *church* youth group party. She asked me one or two questions about Faith Community Fellowship, but I don't remember what they were—probably because I didn't have the answers to her questions! All I remember is that she seemed to get even more quiet after we talked about the church.

Oh, well. We'll just have to see what happens tomorrow.

We got into Collinsville just before two o'clock. We dropped Trish off at her grandmother's house. Mrs. Miller was sure glad to see her. Aunt Beverly went directly to the shop. Dad headed down to the hardware store. Kiersten bounded off to find Mari. And I took a nap!

Kimber came over for a few minutes after supper to show me her new swimsuit. It's a really bright turquoise, which looks great with her black hair. She asked all about Eagle Point and the graduation ceremony. She has her graduation next week from Faith Community School, but there are only about twelve students graduating and most of them haven't been lifelong friends. It will be a little different for her than my graduation was for me. I told her I'd like to come, though, if she wanted me to be there, and she said that would really make her happy. Then when Kimber left, she said something that made me feel really good. She said, "I'm glad you're home, Katelyn."

Home. I never really thought I'd feel that way about Collinsville, but as soon as Kimber said that, I knew she was right. Collinsville *is* home now. It's feeling more like home every day.

Chapter Nine

The Big Splash

I know it's *very* late, but I'm too excited to sleep. I'm writing by the light of the little crystal lamp next to my bed—the one that's only about eight inches high. I hope nobody, meaning Dad, of course, can see light coming from under the door. Dad would want me to get to sleep, but I just *must* tell you about tonight before I forget any of the details.

First, I should tell you that we didn't go to Faith Community Fellowship this morning for church. Instead, we went with Grandpa Stone to the First Baptist Church of Collinsville. Grandpa was feeling better and he was also feeling worse—better in his body, but as he said, "worse in his heart," because he had missed my graduation. I told him that I understood completely, but he still wanted to celebrate in some way. He invited us to go with him to the Manor House for brunch after church, and we decided that it would be easiest if we just went with him to church so we wouldn't have to worry about finding each other. Aunt Beverly was invited to go along, too.

The service was very good. I like Pastor Stevens. He really seems to know his Bible and he's a good preacher. We sang two of the old familiar hymns that we sang at our Baptist church in Eagle Point. Still, I missed seeing Kimber and Jon.

One thing I do really like about the Baptist church is the fact that it *looks* like a church. Faith Community Fellowship is really new. In fact, the place where services are held is actually the gymnasium of Faith Community School. The church decided, Kimber told me, to build the school facilities first and then save for a more formal worship sanctuary. The place where we meet is nice, but it's not very fancy, and anybody looking in wouldn't really know it's a church except for the organ and piano and big cross that's been placed on the east wall.

The First Baptist Church, on the other hand, couldn't be mistaken for anything but a church. In fact, it's just the kind of church I always imagined as a child when I did the little rhyme, "Here's the church, here's the steeple, open the doors, and here are the people." It is white and has a high steeple, and the double doors in front lead into a center aisle that goes all the way to the altar and then the pulpit. The pews have deep blue cushions and the stained glass windows are actually panes of pastel glass cut into squares, and then arched at the top. When the sun shines through the windows during the morning service, it's as if a rainbow is dancing over the pews. When Kiersten was really little, she went chasing the rainbows one morning during the church service. Everybody laughed, but that was probably because everybody wished they could chase the rainbows, too!

The choir sings in front behind the pulpit and the pulpit chairs, which are big old-fashioned chairs with blue tapestry on them. The organ is at the back of the church in the little balcony. The church even has a bell that is rung for services. Like I said, it's just about everything you would imagine a little church should be. Well, a church that's little by comparison, I guess. Grandpa Stone says about a hundred people go there. Years ago, a new Baptist church started out in East Valley and that's really the biggest Baptist church in town, now.

Church was over about 11:30 and we went immediately to the Manor House, which is *the* place to eat in Collinsville. People even drive out from Benton to eat there. It's at the top of the hill on Manor Drive, and it's really just what its name says—an old manor house that's been turned into an inn. The upstairs rooms are made available for weekend stays. Aunt Beverly says they are beautifully decorated and that it's a great honeymoon spot. There's a big swimming pool out back, in a shape that is rather uneven. The pool is surrounded by rocks and plants so it really looks more like a small lake than a swimming pool. There's a fountain that makes a little waterfall flowing into it. Beyond the pool are rose gardens and then a beautiful view of the valley. You can see a lot of the orchard farms, and Grandpa says that on a really clear day, you can see almost as far as Vineland.

On the lower level of the Manor House, all of the rooms have been turned into eating areas—except for the kitchen, of course. You can eat in the library, the great room, the formal dining room, the sunroom, the parlor, or the back porch (which is glassed in). I've only been to the Manor House once before and that time we sat in the great room. This time we were seated in the sunroom, and I really do think it's my favorite. The room is white with lots of real ivy climbing the walls. The chairs are green and white with big deep-rose flowers. The tile on the floor is green. There are paintings on the wall of flowers and there's a little fountain hanging on one wall, with green plants underneath it. The room *felt* like a garden, and that reminded me of Mom. I thought of Mom a lot while we were in Eagle Point. I knew how proud she would have been to see me graduate, and how much she would have loved my dress, and how happy she would have been to see me named Best English Student. As much as I thought about Mom, most of my thoughts were happy thoughts, not sad ones. I'm glad for that.

We had a wonderful lunch and Grandpa gave me a graduation present—a cameo pin that once belonged to my Grandma Stone. I couldn't believe it. A real heirloom! Aunt Beverly said it's one of the finest cameos she's ever seen. Grandpa seemed pleased that I was so pleased. Who wouldn't be? Kiersten kept asking if the person in the cameo was Grandma, and Grandpa said, "I think it just might be." I suspect that he was saying that just to give Kiersten an answer, but in my imagination, I'm going to believe that it is Grandma.

I wish I had more memories of Grandma Stone, especially since I'm named for her . . . partly. Grandma Anna, which is what everybody always calls her, was a very well respected woman in Collinsville. She was president of the Garden Club, and she was also an artist, which is probably where Mom got her talent. Grandma Anna painted fine china. We have a couple of vases, a big bowl, a pitcher, and several cups and saucers she painted. They are truly beautiful. I wish I had inherited the Stone artistic talent, but apparently that all went to Kiersten. She's always been better at drawing and painting than I am, or ever was.

The only real memory I have of Grandma Anna is one when we came to visit and I was probably only four or five years old. Kiersti was just a tiny baby. Grandma Anna made a wonderful lemon cake and I remember that she let me have as many pieces as I wanted. I remember sitting in Grandpa Stone's kitchen with a red-and-white-checkered tablecloth on the whitewashed pine table that Grandpa Stone still has, eating lemon cake, drinking milk, and having Grandma Anna smile at what she called, "a very big appetite for such a beautiful little girl." Mom always said that Grandma Anna loved me a great deal. I was her first granddaughter and I guess that made me extra special. All of which, dear Journal, lets you know just why I am so excited about my new cameo. It's a magnificent present and I need to tell Grandpa Stone that about a hundred more times!

After lunch, we went home and I tried to take a nap, but I was just too excited about the party. Instead of sleeping, I called Libby to make sure that she was still willing to go with Kimber and me, and I also called Trish again. Both Libby and Trish still seemed reluctant, but I finally talked them into a sure "yes."

At six o'clock, Dad drove over to Kimber's to

pick her up, and then we went by to pick up Libby, and then Trish. Kimber had never met Libby, and Trish, of course, hadn't met either Kimber or Libby, so most of the time on the way to the party was spent in introductions. I was glad that neither Kimber nor Trish seemed the least bit concerned that Libby stutters. It's really nice to have such mature friends.

The party was held at the home of the Wilsons. They have a son who is a senior—Tad is his name—and a daughter, Alice, who is a sophomore. I met them both at youth group. They're really nice—friendly to everybody, no matter who you are or what year you are in at CHS. The Wilson home is down by the river—a large old rambling house. The pool is quite a distance from the house. It is fenced all around and has its own pool house.

The Wilsons had set up a barbecue grill and three big picnic tables on the lawn between the house and the pool. Hot dogs were on the grill when we got there.

"You didn't say it was dinner," I whispered to Kimber. "Maybe we should have called to tell them that Libby and Trish were coming."

"I didn't know it was dinner," she whispered back. "The Wilsons are really generous people, though. I'm sure they'll have enough food for everybody."

That might have been the understatement of

the year—at least of the month. There was more food than *two* youth groups could have eaten! They had chips and dip, plenty of hot dog buns and hot dogs, plus several kinds of relish, three different kinds of salads, and then a huge mound of watermelons in big tubs of ice for dessert. Another big tub held dozens of cans of soda pop.

Christian music was playing through stereo speakers by the pool house, and when we got there, several people were already in the pool. Others were standing by the grill waiting for their hot dogs to get done.

"Do you know everybody?" Alice Wilson asked us as she led us out to the backyard.

"Just about," said Kimber. "I think we'll be able to manage." I could tell that Libby and Trish were a little hesitant. "We know each other," I said in a low voice, just loud enough so they could hear me. Both of them smiled. Somehow I really wanted both of them to have a good time. I think I was more concerned about that than about the fact that I knew virtually *nobody* there. Then again, I knew Kimber! It's all a matter of knowing *someone*, I guess.

Oh . . . I forgot to mention that about five o'clock, Aunt Beverly stopped by to help me with my hair and makeup. I think I'm getting the hang of it, but it was nice to have her there to help with the finishing touches. You know, there are some days when your hair just turns out right. There's no predicting it or planning it—it just does. And this afternoon was one of those times. I really felt attractive as we drove to the party, and that attitude must have showed somehow because several people told me within minutes after we had arrived at the party, "You look great tonight."

I know it shouldn't matter how a person looks, but it does. When you know you look OK, you feel more confident and more outgoing, and then the more outgoing you are, the more people respond to you. At least that's the way it seems to work for me.

When we got to the barbecue grill area, I spotted Jon talking to a couple of guys I'd never seen before and I called to him, "Hey, Jon!" He turned around and I would give anything if I had been able to take his photograph at just that moment. His eyes got wide and his mouth dropped open. He just stood there and didn't say a thing for a minute.

"Wow," he finally said. I was relieved to see his grin return. "You look great! It *is* Katelyn Weber, isn't it?"

"You bet," I said.

Quickly Jon turned to his friends and said, "These are two buddies of mine from the gym. This is Dennis Anderson, and this is Julio Martinez."

110

We all said hi and then I introduced Kimber, Libby, and Trish to Jon and his friends.

A funny thing happened as I introduced Jon to Kimber. My tongue got all tangled up, I guess, so what I said came out like this: "Kimber, I'd like for you to meet the Jon Weaver . . . I mean the Weave—I mean Jon." Everybody laughed and so did I. "I've got a great new hairdo and now my mouth won't work," I quipped. I had heard Aunt Beverly use that line just last week.

"The Weave?" said Kimber.

"That's right," said Jon with a *huge* grin. "The Weave."

"The Weave," said Dennis, trying to sound a little macho.

"The Weave," said Julio, trying to be cool.

"Hey, The Weave," said Jon, "by unanimous vote!" He gave me a wink and then said to the side as everybody started talking, "I knew you'd come up with something."

We met a few other people at the party—in fact, before the night was over I think we talked to just about everybody, for at least a minute or two. Most of the evening, though, Kimber, Libby, Trish, and I spent our time eating and then swimming with Jon, Dennis, and Julio. They were a lot of fun to be with and everybody seemed to get along. It almost seemed as if we'd all known each other for a long time.

I knew Jon was really surprised at my new hairstyle and makeup, but I was also in for a couple of surprises. The first surprise was when Jon took off his glasses as we all got ready to jump into the pool. The fact of the matter is, Jon Weaver has fabulous eyes! Not just average eyes, but beautiful eyes, with really long eyelashes. I didn't know glasses could make such a difference—in his case, the difference of hiding his best feature!

The second surprise was when Jon took off his shirt to get ready to swim. I had never really imagined Jon, the computer-science "nerd" that he calls himself, as having muscles. I should have guessed he would, since his dad is the manager of the Collinsville Family Fitness Center, and Jon had said that Dennis and Julio were two of his friends from the gym. Still, it was a shock to see that he wasn't the hundred-pound weakling that I had figured him to be. Those button-down shirts were hiding a major hunk of a guy.

As for me, I really didn't want to get in the pool. I knew that would be the end of my feeling pretty—wet straggly hair and all. But . . . I really had little choice in the matter. Before I knew it, Jon and Dennis had literally picked me up and thrown me in the pool. Fortunately, I had just taken off my skirt and big-shirt top. Once I was all wet, Libby and Trish were willing to get in. I finally convinced Libby that if she didn't like the way she looked in her swimsuit, the best place to be was *in* the water, not sitting on the edge of the pool.

Just about everybody went swimming at some point in the evening, so we were all in the same boat—wet hair and half-washed-off makeup. Nobody seemed to mind, though. It was fun just talking and laughing and playing around in the pool.

About nine o'clock, Bert gathered everybody around one end of the pool and gave a little devotional. He talked about how it's OK for Christians to have fun and that God enjoys watching his children play in an innocent and joyful manner, the same way that parents enjoy watching their little children play and have a good time. I had never thought about that before. Jesus has always seemed a lot more approachable to me than God. That was probably the main reason God sent His Son to the earth. Still, it's a really neat idea to think of God as a loving Father who wants to see His children have good, safe, clean fun.

When Bert was finished with his devotional, we sang a few choruses. Tad and a couple of the other seniors played their guitars. It sounded really neat, especially out there by the pool under the stars. I really didn't want the evening to end. It's probably the first time I have thought that since moving to Collinsville.

While we were singing, I looked over at

Kimber. She had a really sweet smile on her face. I could tell the praise words meant something important to her. The same for Jon. Dennis and Julio I don't know about. They were willing to sing— sorta—but I could tell they didn't know the words so they felt a little awkward. Libby just sat with tears rolling down her cheeks. I wanted to reach over and put my arm around her shoulder, but I think that might have destroyed what the Lord was doing in her heart.

And then I looked at Trish. She was sitting like a stone. No singing. No tears. No expression at all. I sensed that she was working hard to "endure" this part of the party. She had been having such fun when we were goofing around in the pool— she really does have a great personality. Now she looked as if she wanted to run and hide. I hope we can talk about how she feels sometime. Tonight wasn't the night, though.

After the singing ended, we all gathered up our things. I was amazed to realize that it was already ten o'clock, the time we had told Dad we'd be ready to be picked up. He was waiting for us as we walked out. Jon and his friends left the same time we did so I had an opportunity to introduce Jon, Dennis, and Julio to Dad.

"I hear you're a computer whiz," Dad said to Jon.

"I'd like to become one," Jon replied. "Katelyn tells me that I could learn a lot from you."

Dad looked pleased. "You're welcome to come down to Stone's anytime. In fact, you may be able to help us with some things this summer. Do you have a summer job lined up?"

"Well, I have one possibility, but I may be able to change my plans," Jon said.

"Come down next week and let's talk," Dad said.

I was in shock. That would be something—Jon working at Stone's Hardware!

Kimber and Libby and Trish and I didn't say much on the way home. The drive to Trish's house was just a couple of minutes. Libby said she had a good time. And Kimber, much to my surprise, admitted that she was absolutely smitten with Dennis. I hadn't even noticed! Where was I?

It will be fun to see what happens! I hope Dennis and Julio will start coming to youth group. Libby and Trish, too. Libby, I think, can be talked into it. I'm not so sure about Trish.

Perhaps the best part of the evening was that I really felt comfortable with everyone who was there. That's one of the best things about groups of Christian kids, I think. It's easier to feel as if you have something in common. Nobody was a snob or mean.

There was one strange moment, though.

Two little white dogs came running into the Wilsons' yard, and shortly after that, a girl in a white dress came running after them, a leash in each hand. She seemed very apologetic about her dogs spoiling the party. I asked Kimber if she knew who she was and she said she didn't. For some reason, I felt as if I knew her. Maybe I've seen her in the hall at school.

I'll have to watch for her.

Goodnight for now, Journal. It was a great day!

Chapter Ten

Expert
Advice

Wednesday
8 P.M.

I can't believe it's already the last week of school—well, sorta. On my first day at Collinsville High, I thought the end of the term seemed an eternity away. Now I wonder where the time went. Next Monday is the last day of school, but graduation for the seniors is Friday night. Monday is supposedly set aside for us to figure out our schedules for the fall term, sign up for classes, clean out our lockers, and things like that.

Several important things have happened already this week. I've just been too busy to sit down and write much about them.

First, Kimber, Trish, Libby, and two girls named Marcia and Sam (short for Samantha) are going to have a slumber party on Saturday night at Kimber's house. Marcia and Sam are Kimber's two best friends at her school. Kimber's graduation is Friday night, so Saturday is her private graduation party. I've already picked out a present for her at Aunt Beverly's shop—a couple of those little silver frames and a blank book so she can start her own journal. She saw my journal Monday night and asked me about it. Kimber is more into math and music than writing, but she said she thought writing in a journal might help her enjoy writing more. I encouraged her to give it a try.

So . . . I have another party on the horizon. I'm hoping that Trish will open up to us a little during the slumber party. Sometimes it's easier to talk when the lights are out and everybody is in a good mood.

The second big news of the week is that Mr. Clark Weaver—Mr. Wonderful Customer himself—has asked Aunt Beverly to give him some advice on how he might decorate his house. I think it's a lame excuse for a date, but Aunt Beverly seemed pleased that he asked her to come over and make some suggestions. Aunt Beverly said he came into the shop last Saturday morning, and when Mrs. Campbell told him that we were away until noon, he left without buying anything and said he'd be back. (I've been telling Aunt Beverly that the main reason he comes to the shop is to see her, but she has pretended not to believe me!) Anyway . . . he showed up just a few minutes before closing and, according to Aunt Beverly, his exact words were, "I really like the way your shop *feels*. It has a warm feeling, without being too fussy or frilly. That's the way I'd like for my living room to feel, but I don't know how you made the shop feel this way. Do you suppose you might come over sometime and give me some decorating advice?"

"Great!" I said when Aunt Beverly told me that.

She smiled a weak little smile and then added, "But *then* he said, 'I'd want to pay you, of course, for your services.'"

"Oh, no!" I said. "He wants to *hire* you? That's not very romantic."

"That's what I thought," said Aunt Beverly. "Maybe it really is the shop that is attractive to him, and not me."

"What did you say?" I asked her.

"I just laughed a little and said we'll see," she replied.

Anyway . . . Aunt Beverly is going over to Mr. Clark Weaver's house on Sunday afternoon to see what she can see. I can hardly wait to hear what the house is like. I have a hunch it's a real bachelor's pad.

Aunt Beverly seems excited about the idea. I'm glad for that. It's been a long time since she dated—since Ellory McKay, as a matter of fact. At least as far as I know. I liked Ellory, but he was a rather strange guy in some ways. Forty-something. He'd never been married and he really did have some eccentricities. For one thing, he rode a bicycle everywhere. Aunt Beverly said he had a car, but I never saw him in one. He even rode his bicycle to Benton, and that's thirty-five miles away. Aunt Beverly said he was into long-distance cycling and that he had once cycled all the way across the state in a relay. Another strange thing about Ellory was that he spoke with an accent and used lots of unusual phrases. I thought that was pretty weird at first, but then Aunt Beverly told me that his mother was from Scotland and that he had grown up spending his summers with his aunts and uncles there.

Well, so much for old Ellory. Aunt Beverly finally gave up on him, I think. One day he just rode off into the sunset—on his bike, of course—and I haven't seen him since. When I asked Aunt Beverly about it, she simply said, "Some things just aren't meant to be for a lifetime." I don't think she was particularly sad. I think it was more that she'd lost somebody to go places with.

Even though I don't know that much about Mr. Clark Weaver, I think he's more her type. Especially if he likes the shop so much.

But now for the two biggies of the week—at least so far. Number one: Jon went in to see Dad on Monday afternoon and the result is that Jon is going to work part-time at Stone's Hardware this summer. He's also going to work part-time at Collinsville Family Fitness Center, where his dad is the manager. He'll spend the mornings at Stone's, helping Dad set up an inventory system on the computer, and his afternoons at the Fitness Center—get this, teaching golf and skeet shooting. I had no idea that Jon Weaver could do either! He really is a guy with lots of surprises. I'm curious to find out how he learned to skeet shoot. Grandpa Stone used to enjoy that sport. I don't know anybody in our family who plays golf, though. Maybe I could learn to play.

Dad said something really neat about Jon after he had been in the store. He said, "That boy has real potential. He's going to be a computer expert someday. I just may learn a thing or two from him."

The last of the big news is something that Jon said to me. He asked me if he could walk me home from school yesterday, so I waited for him at the entrance after phys ed class was over. When he didn't show, I wandered over to the computer lab, where I found him working on a problem in the accounting program that the business students use.

Miss Scaroni saw me and after Jon introduced me to her, she said, "You're the girl, aren't you, who got the best of those guys in the hall a couple of weeks ago?"

"Yes," I grinned. "I hope I didn't embarrass you."

"Embarrass me? No way," she said. "I think you embarrassed them, though. They've been model students ever since, although they don't seem particularly friendly toward Jon."

"That's OK," said Jon. "You can't be friends with everybody."

"You've got a good attitude about that, Jon," said Miss Scaroni. "I really appreciate your help in getting this program untangled. Some of the business students *think* they know more about how to manipulate some of these programs than they actually do."

"Glad I could help," said Jon as he shut off the computer.

"I hope I don't embarrass *you*, Jon," Miss Scaroni continued, "but I've wanted to say something to you for several weeks now."

"Go ahead," said Jon. "Katelyn's just about my best friend here at school. I don't mind her hearing."

"I really admire you, Jon," said Miss Scaroni. "You aren't afraid to be your best and to do your best, even though that may not always be appreciated by your peers. It really takes a lot of courage to go for excellence when other people are willing to settle for average. I believe you're going to go far in life, not just in computers, but in anything you try."

Jon grinned—I could tell he was grinning even though I didn't look at him. Miss Scaroni extended her hand and Jon reached out and shook it heartily. "Thanks, Miss Scaroni," he said. "I've really enjoyed your class."

"Will you be taking Advanced Computing next year?" she asked.

"If you'll let me in the class," said Jon.

"There's no question," she said.

At that, Jon and I left.

"*Almost* your best friend," I teased Jon as we walked down the hall. "And here I thought I was your best friend without qualification!"

"Actually, you are—" said Jon . . . but I cut him off.

"That's OK. You don't have to explain," I teased. And then more seriously, I added, "That was really great—what Miss Scaroni said to you. She gave you a real compliment. Dad said something along those same lines after he met with you on Monday."

"Oh, they're just being nice," said Jon. *Now* he seemed a little embarrassed.

"I don't think that's it," I said. "I think Dad and Miss Scaroni genuinely meant what they said. You've got a lot of talent and you're going to go far in life."

"It means a lot for you to say that, Katelyn," said Jon. He didn't seem very happy, though, as he spoke.

"Is something wrong?" I asked.

"Well, I seem to impress adults, all right. My teachers have always given me a lot of encouragement and praise. I just don't seem to be able to do so well in getting my classmates to like me."

"Do you really feel that way, Jon?" I asked. I was a bit surprised to hear him say that.

"Yeah, I do," he said, and it almost sounded like a confession. "I wish I could make friends as easily as you do."

"Me?" I said. "I'm a big scaredy-cat when it comes to meeting new people."

"Hardly," said Jon. "Just look. You've already got three great friends—Kimber, Libby, Trish. Dennis and Julio thought you were great. All the kids at the swim party were eager to talk to you, and I've noticed that lots and lots of kids say hi to you when they pass you in the hall."

"Things have gone a lot better here than I ever thought they would," I admitted.

"And me?" Jon continued. "Dennis and Julio are friends I work out with at the gym, but I'm just barely getting to know them. There's only so much you can say when you're trying to lift weights. I may be an expert in computers, but I think I need some expert help in knowing how to be a better friend."

I didn't really know what to say so I didn't say anything. Jon didn't seem to notice my silence. After a couple of moments he said, "I also like the way you take risks, Katelyn."

"Risks?" I asked.

"Sure," he said. "Just look at the way you changed your looks—overnight! You left school on Thursday looking—well, pretty—but then you showed up at the party on Sunday looking like a super model!"

"Hardly!" I laughed. "It's amazing what a few curls and a little makeup can do."

"Yeah," he said, "it may seem like a little thing to you, but I was really impressed that you were willing to try a new look."

"Don't you like the way you look?" I asked, suddenly having an outlandish idea that maybe, just maybe, Jon Weaver was in the market for an Aunt Beverly make-over!

"Not particularly," said Jon.

"Well, I know just the person who can give you some expert advice!" I said.

"Who?" he asked.

"My Aunt Beverly. She's coming over to your house on Sunday afternoon anyway. Did you know that?"

"Dad said something about a decorator coming over. He didn't say who," Jon said.

"Well, it's Aunt Beverly he's calling his decorator! Maybe I could come with her and we could both talk to her about what you'd like to change."

"I'd be too embarrassed," said Jon.

"I don't think so—at least not once you met Aunt Beverly," I said. "You weren't too embarrassed to say this to me."

"That's because you're my friend," said Jon with a grin.

"Yeah," I said. "*Almost* your best one at CHS."

With that, I raced up the walk to the house and called to Jon from the step on the porch, "Think about Sunday!"

I know I'm already thinking about it, Journal. It would really be fun to see just how handsome Jon Weaver could become!

Chapter Eleven

Mapping Out a Plan

Sunday
8 P.M.

*W*ithout a doubt, this has been the biggest weekend of my life—at least since coming to Collinsville.

Friday was Kimber's graduation and it really was neat. The ceremony was held in the main auditorium at Faith Community Fellowship. All of the graduates—girls, that is—wore white dresses. The girls were allowed to choose different styles, but the dresses had to be all white, or nearly all white. Kimber's dress was really pretty. It was very straight, and had a dropped waist, with a gathered skirt that came just to the top of her knees and a plain top. The dress had a high neckline and was sleeveless. It was made of real silk and the straight style really showed off her slender figure. She had pulled her hair up into a truly elegant style, with big round curls that looked like they were pretty heavily moussed. I'm going to have to ask her how she did that. She looked like a model straight out of *Seventeen* magazine.

The school bought red rose corsages for all the graduating girls. The corsages were trimmed in navy blue ribbon—the school colors are navy and red. That was a really neat idea. The boys had red carnation boutonnieres. (They wore white shirts and navy and red ties.)

Pastor Rogers spoke and encouraged the graduates to take their Christian values with them as they entered various high schools in the area. The seniors sang the school song together, and after the diplomas were handed out, the parents were invited to come forward and to put their arms around their own graduates while Pastor Rogers led everybody in a prayer. It was a really special time.

As far as I know, Kimber is the only graduating girl from Faith Community Fellowship who is going to attend Collinsville High School next fall. Nearly all of the students will be going to East Valley High—which is over on the east side of Collinsville, a newer part of town. East Valley is the rival high school to Collinsville. I guess that makes sense since it's the only other high school in town.

Kimber felt about her graduation the same way

I did, in some ways. She's leaving her friends and starting out at a new school. She's a little scared. (I know that feeling!) Collinsville High is much much larger than the school she just graduated from. But at least for her, she has Libby and me as friends going into Collinsville High. It's kinda neat how God arranged things, I think. Kimber helped me break the ice at Faith Community Fellowship and the youth group, and I'll be able to help her in high school. I guess that's what friends are for!

Anyway . . . after the ceremony, the graduates had a reception like we did for everybody who was present, and they also had a photographer. (The ivy-covered archway he used as a setting looked just the same as the one we had at Eagle Point!) The graduates, though, didn't really have a party by themselves. They will be going on an overnight trip next weekend called "The Senior Fling." They are going to—get this—Castle Rock! There's going to be a Christian concert there at the outdoor amphitheater and they're going to attend that, and before the concert they're going to have a big cook-out on the beach. Sounds like fun.

The Chans seemed really pleased for Kimber, and Kiersten and Mari were her private cheering section. They didn't yell or anything, but they sure waved at Kimber a lot and gave her huge smiles. It's easy to see that Mari really adores Kimber. The two of them get along a lot like Kiersten and

I do, except that Kimber is probably more patient with Mari than I am with Kiersten. (It *could* have something to do with the fact that Mari doesn't ask nearly a tenth of the questions that Kiersten asks!)

At the reception I got to meet Marcia and Sam. I was glad for the chance to meet them before the slumber party.

Then on Saturday morning I worked at Aunt Beverly's. Who should come in, of course, but Mr. Clark Weaver! This time I felt really brave and while Aunt Beverly was pouring him a complimentary cup of decaffeinated Jamocha and Cream coffee, I went over and said to him, "Mr. Weaver, my name is Katelyn."

"Of course," he said. "Your aunt introduced me to you the last time I saw you in the shop. You look a lot more grown up this week, though."

"Thanks," I said.

He went on, "You talked me into those candles, remember?"

"Yes, I remember," I said. "I hope you like them."

"Oh, I do," he said.

He seemed willing enough to talk, so I went on to say, "I don't know whether you know it or not, but your son, Jon, is a good friend of mine."

"He's told me a lot about you, actually," said Mr. Clark Weaver. "He thinks you're the nicest

130

person he's met at Collinsville High. In fact, I think he said something about your coming over with Beverly—I mean, your Aunt Beverly—tomorrow afternoon. Is that right?"

"Well, if it's OK with you and Aunt Beverly. Jon and I wanted to talk to Aunt Beverly about a little project, and it seemed to be a good time to get together."

"Fine with me," said Mr. Clark Weaver. "Your aunt and I were just discussing the time. Will three o'clock be all right with you?"

"Perfect," I said.

Then Mr. Clark Weaver said something that really woke me up. "You know, Katelyn, this whole decorating idea is mostly your fault." *Fault? Oh no,* the thought raced through my mind, *have I done something wrong?*

"My fault?" I said with hesitation.

He said, "Yes. If you hadn't talked me into those blue candles I might never have given decorating much of a thought. But when I got those candles home, I realized I had no candle holders in the house. So I had to come back and get some candle holders. And then when I got them home, I realized that I didn't have a table on which to put those candles. So—you really started something."

"S-o-o-o sorry," I teased. I figured if he was at all like Jon, he could take a little teasing.

"Well, we should know more about the full

extent of how sorry you should be after tomorrow, I guess, when your Aunt Beverly tells me all that I *don't* have and need to purchase," said Mr. Clark Weaver with the predictable Weaver grin.

After Mr. Clark Weaver left the shop, Aunt Beverly seemed to lose a little of her ability to concentrate. I caught her in two math errors at the cash register, and that isn't at all like Aunt Beverly. I think she's really looking forward to Sunday—more than she was willing to admit to me.

On Saturday evening, I went to Kimber's house about eight o'clock, which is when she had invited us to come over. Marcia was already there, and shortly after I arrived, Libby and Sam came. It was nearly nine o'clock, though, before Trish showed up. I have a hunch she was struggling with second thoughts, but we were all glad to see her, and she got acquainted with Marcia and Sam very quickly. To some people, Trish may even seem to come on too strong, but I like her bold approach a lot. I wish I could be more like her. Trish is quick to speak and can talk easily about lots of things. Libby says she is very "spontaneous."

There's an interesting thing about Libby that I've learned in the last week. She has a *great* vocabulary. That seemed a little strange to me at first because she stutters, but when I complimented her on all the words she knows, she gave me a perfectly understandable explanation, "If you're going to make people w-w-w-wait to hear a w-w-w-word, it might as well be a word worth waiting for." And then she laughed. "That's a lot of W's for a s-s-s-s-stutterer!" It made me really glad to see that Libby trusted me enough to laugh about her stuttering. That was a far cry from the first day I met her!

I just realized that I haven't told you very much about the way Libby and Trish look. Libby is shorter than I am—about the same height as Kimber. She has dark hair and is about average in build. She talks a lot about being overweight, but I think it's more her body type. She's part Italian and she has a pretty face, with big dark eyes. She has an olive-colored complexion. Libby likes to wear really loose tops—like giant T-shirts—and full, rather longish skirts. She really likes to wear sandals. She pulls the top part of her hair back in a very casual style. Overall, I'd say her look is very "relaxed."

Trish, on the other hand, is very pulled together. She is shorter than either Libby or Kimber and has short blond hair that's really thick, but pretty fine. She likes to mousse it and just run her fingers through it, and she pretty much gets away with that look. None of the rest of us could!

Trish has a very athletic look about her. She doesn't wear any makeup, except occasionally she'll wear really bright lipstick. She likes sports,

133

especially baseball. She has a whole collection of baseball-style hats—some of which are pretty wild in their colors and designs. She likes to wear T-shirts, too, but ones that fit and show off her cute figure. So far, I've never seen her in anything other than a jeans skirt or jeans shorts . . . with a T-shirt. Her style is *super* casual, but in a very different way from Libby's.

On slumber party night, of course, we all were casual. And before long, we had to laugh at ourselves. We had all pulled our hair up into ponytails (except Trish, whose hair isn't long enough for that), and we all had changed into very big nightshirt-style T-shirts. Different styles by day . . . but very similar styles by night!

We talked and ate our way to ten o'clock, doing each other's hair and experimenting with makeup. I learned a lot of neat new tricks from Kimber and Sam—who is really into makeup. We had the most fun making up Libby, who has hardly ever worn *any* makeup. By the time we got done with her, she hardly recognized herself. It definitely wasn't a daytime look, however. She looked like she was twenty and ready for a date in Benton.

At ten o'clock, we started what turned out to be something of a marathon video show—two full tapes of *Anne of Avonlea*. I had seen them before, several years ago—along with the first part of the series, *Anne of Green Gables*—but it was really fun to see them again. Such a romantic, nice story—with a happy ending for a change. And in all, just about four hours of watching! We had time outs for making popcorn, of course.

The videos lasted until almost two-thirty in the morning, when we all got a second wind and had a rip-roaring pillow fight. Then, it was down to some serious boy talk. I've never really enjoyed boy talk before, but this time it seemed different. Kimber has a huge crush on Dennis and I was able to tell her a little more about Dennis after talking to Jon. The news she wanted to hear, of course, was that Dennis is also interested in her! Talk about one excited Kimberly Chan! I think that was the best graduation present she received!

(I didn't tell you about Kimber's presents. Marcia and Sam had gone in together to give her a silver bracelet—the kind you can add charms to. On it they put a charm of a graduation cap and diploma, and also "M" and "S" charms—to remind Kimber, they said, of them. Libby gave her a pretty box of stationery that she had picked out at Aunt Beverly's shop. Trish gave her a bright yellow baseball hat with a big orange "K" on it. She really liked my gifts—the frames and journal I already wrote about.)

While we were deep into boy talk, Trish shocked us all by saying that she thought the greatest guy at the swim party had been Tad Wilson. "But he's a senior!" Libby, Kimber, and I said in unison.

She said, "Thank you, back-up singers, thank you very much," and we all rolled over in laughter. Trish has some great one-liners sometimes.

Marcia and Sam know Tad, too, so it was easy for all of us to talk about what it would be like to date a person who had just *finished* high school, and what we thought Trish's chances were of even getting his attention. Actually, I think they might be pretty good. She's got just the personality to make an older guy notice her.

I was glad nobody brought up the subject of Jon Weaver. I really wouldn't have known what to say about Jon. He's a great friend and I wouldn't have wanted to say anything that would have put him down or made light of our friendship, but at the same time, I don't want anybody to think that he's a boyfriend.

We all wondered how we could get to know Dennis and Julio and some of the other guys at the party and at school a little better. Getting to know boys is so much more difficult than getting to know girls.

And about then is when Libby said, "I'm just g-g-g-glad that you all are my f-f-f-friends."

"That's it!" I nearly shouted. A truly incredible idea had just popped into my head with such a rush I could hardly contain it.

"That's what?" they all asked me—again in unison.

I picked up on Trish's line and said, "Thank you, choir, thank you."

"We need a club," I said.

"A club?" said Marcia. "You mean like with a tree house?"

"Only ours would say, 'Boys allowed'!" said Trish. Like I said, she's very quick witted.

"Not exactly," I said. But when Libby said what she did, the idea hit me. "Why not have a club where we can all just be friends and we don't have to worry about guys and girls being together as couples, or about who likes whom? We can just hang out together as friends."

"What would we call it?" asked Kimber.

"F-f-friends Club?" said Libby.

"That's it!" I said.

"What?" said Trish. "Friends Club? A little generic, don't you think?"

"No," I said and I could hardly stop grinning. "The first part of what Libby said. FF!"

Libby groaned, but she was also smiling. I don't think she minded at all being teased a little.

"FF?" said Kimber.

"Yeah, as in Friend Flips out," said Trish.

"Or, Faithful Friends," said Marcia.

"Or, Fantastic Future," said Sam.

Everybody was getting into the act. Kimber

suggested "Food and Fun" but then she added, "Katelyn probably means Faith and Fellowship." Libby said, "How about Found a Friend?"

Marcia offered a second suggestion, "Forged in Faith," and Sam picked up on that to say, "Friends in Faith."

"That's the great thing about it!" I said. "FF can mean lots of things. We could keep people guessing. What I actually had in mind was Forever Friends!"

Well, we spent the next hour talking about what the FF Club might do and be, but we were so punchy by that hour—it was nearly five o'clock—that we decided we should probably have a meeting about it after Kimber, Marcia, and Sam get back from their trip next weekend. We did decide, however, that the main point of the club should be to help out in the community in some way, and not be just a social club. We all agreed that guys and girls can have lots of fun together when they're working on a project—even more fun than at a party sometimes.

One part of our conversation has haunted me a little bit since Saturday night—well, actually, early Sunday morning. At one point, Trish asked if the group would be different from the youth group at Faith Community Fellowship.

"Well, I think it should be," I said. "Youth group is youth group."

"I'm glad," she said.

I probably should have asked her right then and there what she meant, but instead I went on to say, "I think it should be a group in which any high school student in Collinsville could come and be a part—regardless of what church or school he goes to. Surely there are some kids at Collinsville High who are Christians, but who don't go to Faith Community Fellowship—or even First Baptist, for that matter. This should be a club where everybody can get together without it being tied to one church."

"Isn't there a group like that?" asked Kimber. "Marcia, doesn't your sister belong to a group called Young Life?"

"Yeah," said Marcia. "There's a group at East Valley, but they meet mostly for Bible study and parties, and sometimes they go to Benton to hear special speakers."

"Is there a Young Life group at Collinsville?" I asked. Nobody knew . . . natcherly. I'm the one who has been at Collinsville High the longest and I've only been going there four weeks!

"Well, this group still might be different," I said. "Especially if it included kids from all parts of Collinsville, and was organized by kids, for kids."

"That will take a lot of work," said Trish.

We all agreed on that point, and as I said, it was late—or very early, depending on your perspective—and we decided to meet later to talk about details.

I'm really excited, Journal, about this possibility. Lots of thoughts raced through my head, but they must have worn me out because the next thing I knew, I was waking up to the smell of bacon and french toast. Mrs. Chan fixed a wonderful breakfast for us—which we managed to eat about eight o'clock. Which, in turn, meant that we really had to scramble to get ready to go home and still try to make it to church. As it turned out, Kimber and I were the only ones who showed up. Libby and Trish both told me later that they had gone home and crashed into bed—they were so sleepy. The same for Marcia and Sam.

I was sleepy, too, but the thought of what was going to happen on Sunday afternoon kept me going.

And with that, I think I'm going to have to call it a night. I'm really sleepy now. . . .

I'll tell you about Sunday afternoon at Jon's house next time. Maybe I can get up extra early in the morning and write.

Chapter Twelve

Redecorating

*J*ust as I suspected, I awoke bright and early this morning—very early. I think I have just about enough time to write about yesterday afternoon before I have to get ready for school. It helps that we don't start school today until ten o'clock. The entire day has a special schedule, mostly a series of sessions to get us organized and ready for next fall.

Back to yesterday. Aunt Beverly came by to pick me up at 2:30—which seemed really early to me since Jon only lives two blocks up the street—but Aunt Beverly said she had a couple of stops to make first. To get "housewarming presents," she said. Our first stop was at the shop, where we packed up a big glass pitcher and set of glasses, and also a glazed cachepot. I noticed that Aunt

141

Beverly had made a big jug of lemonade. I could see her plan coming together. That would be her excuse for giving Mr. Clark Weaver a set of glasses and a beautiful pitcher. And then on the way we stopped by Jacobs Grocery and got a green plant for the cachepot. "Something for each of us to carry and give," said Aunt Beverly.

We got to Jon's house at just a few minutes after three o'clock, and both he and his dad, Mr. Clark Weaver, were sitting on the porch waiting for us.

They seemed genuinely pleased with the presents. I hadn't realized that Aunt Beverly had also prepared a big box of homemade cookies—oatmeal cookies, mostly—some with chocolate chips and some with butterscotch chips. My favorites!

Jon and I took the cookies and lemonade into the kitchen while Aunt Beverly and Mr. Clark Weaver began to talk in the living room.

The house—at least what I saw of it—was pretty much as I had imagined it would be. Everything very practical, but not particularly beautiful. At least it was clean and things were in good repair.

While Jon and I were in the kitchen, I told him a little about the idea for the FF Club. He picked up on it right away. "I can't imagine that a guy wouldn't want to belong to a Fabulous Females club," he said. "Or a club devoted to Flicks and Food."

"It's a *service* club," I said.

"Great," he said with a grin. "I can serve with girls."

"It's a club for *Christians*," I said.

"Great," he said again, his grin just getting bigger. "I can especially like being around Christian girls."

"It's a club for *friends*," I said.

"Even more great," he said. "Christian girl friends sounds just about right to me!"

"You're impossible," I said, knowing that he was teasing me. "You just may not be allowed in."

"I thought you said that membership would be open to all kids who wanted to do a community service project together," said Jon.

"I did," I teased. "But we haven't come up with *all* the rules yet."

At that point, we joined Aunt Beverly and Mr. Clark Weaver in the living room . . . just in time to hear Aunt Beverly ask, "Would you be willing to move some of the furniture you have?"

"Sure," said Mr. Clark Weaver. "Just tell us where."

He and Jon rolled up their sleeves, and under Aunt Beverly's direction, they moved the sofa away from the wall and parallel to the fireplace. Then they moved the chair ninety degrees to the sofa so that the chair and sofa formed what Aunt Beverly called a "grouping" in front of the fireplace.

Next, Aunt Beverly asked Mr. Clark Weaver about various things that he might have—such as a coffee table, an end table, and so forth. They began to make lists and then to talk about curtains and rugs. Jon and I looked at each other and headed for the front porch.

"Your aunt has a lot of good ideas," said Jon.

"She has *great* ideas," I said. "I'm always amazed at what she comes up with."

"Do you really think she'll take me on as a client?" he asked.

"No," I said, without any expression. "I don't think she'll take you on as a client."

"Oh," he said, sounding a little disappointed.

"I do think she'll give you some ideas as a *friend*," I said.

Jon grinned. "Let's talk a little more about the FF Club."

"OK," I said, "but what I'd really like to talk to you about is Trish."

"Trish?" he said. "What about Trish?"

"I'm really wondering if she knows the Lord," I said.

"How do you mean?" he asked.

I told him what I had noticed at the swim party and about what she said at the slumber party last night.

"Maybe she just isn't very open about her faith," Jon said. "I think a lot of people are like that. I find it difficult sometimes to talk about God or to tell people what Jesus means to me."

"But you are a Christian, aren't you, Jon?" I asked. I was really pretty surprised at myself. I don't think I've ever asked a person that question before. Somehow, though, it seemed natural to ask Jon that, especially since I was pretty sure of the answer.

"Yes," said Jon.

Just at that moment, Aunt Beverly and Mr. Clark Weaver came out on the porch carrying a plate of cookies, the pitcher of lemonade, and a tray of glasses filled with ice.

"Yes, what?" asked Aunt Beverly.

"Jon and I were just talking about the Lord," I said.

"Sunday night testimony time," said Mr. Clark Weaver.

"Oh, you had that, too?" said Aunt Beverly.

"What are you talking about?" I asked, as Jon said at the same time, "Testimony time?"

"Sure," said Aunt Beverly. "On Sunday nights at church—way back when I was a lot younger than you two—we used to have a 'testimony time.' Various people in the congregation would stand and tell what the Lord meant to them, or how the Lord had answered their prayers. It was great."

"It built up your faith, too," said Mr. Clark Weaver. "At least in my life, I felt less weird about some of the spiritual experiences I was having as a kid, and as a teen-ager. If other people loved God and were open about saying so, then it was easier for me somehow."

"I know what you mean," said Aunt Beverly.

"Well, I'm not saying it particularly well," said Mr. Clark Weaver, "but let's just leave it like this: testimony time was always interesting, and it was always good."

"We could have our own testimony time right now!" said Aunt Beverly. When she said that, Journal, a part of me flipped a little inside. Aunt Beverly can be really bold sometimes. I wasn't at all sure I wanted to do what I suspected she had in mind. But . . . it turned out OK.

"You start," said Mr. Clark Weaver, pointing toward Aunt Beverly.

"Well," Aunt Beverly began, "I can testify that the Lord has given me a lot of peace and a feeling of fulfillment in my life. Before I came to know Him, I didn't really know who I was or why God had made me. I didn't feel as if I was a major sinner—I was a pretty good kid as a teen-ager— but I did feel empty inside, as if something was missing in my life. I went to church regularly with my parents and Katelyn's father, but there was a general sense of dissatisfaction I had, even though I couldn't pinpoint it or describe it.

"Then, in college, my best friend Elizabeth—

Katelyn's mother—asked me to go to church with her one night. It was during what the Baptist church called a 'revival week.' The preacher explained what it meant to be saved—to accept what Jesus did on the Cross as being just for you, and to ask the Lord to forgive you of your sins and to help you build a relationship with Him. I knew that I needed what the pastor was describing, so I went forward and knelt at the altar there in the church that was right next door to McKinney College. I prayed and I can't explain what happened, but when I finished praying, I knew that the Lord was not only my Savior, but my Friend. My life felt full and whole. I've had a sense of God's peace in my life ever since, even through some rough times."

"That's the way I felt, too," I said. I couldn't *believe* it was me talking. "I experienced just about the same thing, Aunt Beverly, two years ago at the youth camp I attended over in Castle Rock." I had never heard Aunt Beverly give her testimony before and I was surprised that she had felt so much the way I had felt.

"It really made a difference in your life, didn't it?" Aunt Beverly asked, knowing the answer, of course.

"Oh, yes," I said. "Before that week at camp I was pretty rebellious against Mom and Dad. I was only twelve but I really thought I knew it all. I think it was just that I didn't know who I was, so I was trying to cover up my own insecurity. I don't know what would have happened if I hadn't invited the Lord into my life. I can't imagine going through Mom's death or the move to Collinsville without knowing that the Lord was going to help me."

"What about you, Clark?" asked Aunt Beverly.

"Well, I came to know the Lord about six years ago," said Mr. Clark Weaver. "I was a lot older than you gals when I made my decision to accept Jesus as my Savior. Jon's mother had died a few years before, and after she died, I felt so empty inside that all I could think about was trying to get away from the pain. I packed up little Jon and hit the road for a few years. I think I felt that as long as I was moving, I wouldn't have to face the emptiness I felt inside. But then"—and at that, Mr. Clark Weaver reached over to tousle Jon's hair—"old Jon here needed to go to school so I had to settle down.

"A man named Mr. Simpson was our next-door neighbor and he became a real friend to me. He told me about the loss of his wife to cancer and how the Lord helped him through the dark times he had felt. He got me into reading the Bible and finally, I agreed to go to church with him. One night, I said to him, 'Jerry, I think I'm ready to invite God into my life.' He led me in a very simple sinner's prayer, and I just turned all my hurt and emptiness over to God. I can't explain what happened, but it was as if God just poured Himself into that empty place in my heart and gave me a big dose of joy. I began to laugh out loud—for the first time in years, really."

"And I'll bet you've been grinning ever since," said Aunt Beverly. We all laughed. A grin and a Weaver just seem to go together.

"What about you, Jon?" asked Aunt Beverly. I held my breath. It was one thing for Aunt Beverly to put me on the spot. It was another thing for her to do that to Jon. I hoped Jon didn't feel too embarrassed.

"I think it was the laughing that got my attention," said Jon. "I don't think I had ever heard my dad laugh out loud before. Not that I remembered, at least. I was only eight years old at the time, but I knew that something had really happened in his life. Before that, Dad had been fun—more like in an adventuresome way—but now he really seemed to enjoy life. I asked him what had happened to make him so happy and he told me. I said, 'Can I pray with Mr. Simpson, too?' Dad said, 'Sure,' and we went right over to Mr. Simpson's house."

"You were so young," said Aunt Beverly. "Did your prayer really mean something to you?"

"Yeah, it did," said Jon. "I knew as I was praying that my life was going to be different from that point on. Dad's life had changed, so I expected my life to change, too."

"Tell them what the prayer was that you prayed," said Mr. Clark Weaver.

"Well, Mr. Simpson had me repeat lines after him and I still remember the prayer. It had only four lines. 'God, this is Jon. Thank you for sending Jesus to show me what You are like. I accept what He did on the Cross for me. I want You to be my heavenly Father and I want to be Your son.'"

"What a great prayer," said Aunt Beverly. I thought so, too. It brought tears to my eyes.

"Down through the years, I've repeated that prayer a couple of times. Each time, it has meant more to me. The important thing is that I know He *is* my heavenly Father and I am one of His sons."

"Amen," I said. It seemed the right thing to say in a testimony time, and Mr. Clark Weaver and Aunt Beverly also joined in with "amens."

Aunt Beverly stood to pour some more lemonade all around, and as she did, she said, "I'm glad to know that about you, Jon."

He just nodded as she filled his glass. Aunt Beverly went on, "Katelyn tells me that you would like to have a new 'look,' sort of like what Katelyn did a couple of weeks ago."

"Really?" said Mr. Clark Weaver.

"Well, I thought it might be fun to try something new," said Jon.

"Your own redecorating job, huh?" he said, teasing Jon.

"Yeah, except that I don't want to move any sofas around," replied Jon.

"Redecorating is really the important word to keep in mind," said Aunt Beverly. "I've talked to people in the past who want to redecorate their houses and in doing so, they think they are going to create a home. It doesn't work that way. A house only feels as cozy as the relationships between the people who live there. And the same goes for a new look."

Aunt Beverly began passing the cookies around as she continued, "I don't think I would have suggested a new look to Katelyn unless I had been sure that she knew who she was on the inside. A new look on the *outside* of a person doesn't make the person new on the inside. Only the Lord can do that. A new look can help *reveal* who is really inside, but it can never create a new spirit."

"That's a good point," said Mr. Clark Weaver.

"I agree," said Jon. "I know that some of the changes I'd like to see in my life aren't going to be solved with a new haircut."

"As long as you know that," said Aunt Beverly, "you can relax and have fun experimenting. Let's see what you look like without your glasses."

151

Jon took off his glasses and faked a couple of model-like poses for Aunt Beverly. I could see the wheels really turning in her head.

"I've been thinking about getting contacts," Jon said. "I've been saving up the money I make at the gym."

"If you want contacts, I'll buy those for you, Jon," said Mr. Clark Weaver. "Use your money for whatever else Beverly might suggest."

"Do you have to work this week?" Aunt Beverly asked.

"Well, we have school on Monday," Jon said. "But my summer jobs don't start until the following Monday. I have off Tuesday through Friday."

"Great," said Aunt Beverly as she started picking up the empty glasses and pitcher.

And that, Journal, brings you up to this very hour. I'd better hurry if I'm going to get to school on time!

Chapter Thirteen

Emily's
Place

*W*ell, the school year is officially over, and what an ending it had.

Jon and Libby and I were busy all day turning in our books, cleaning out our lockers, and trying to make sense of our schedules for next fall.

The morning began with an assembly during which Dr. Collins, the principal, described the registration forms we were all to fill out. Each student was supposed to chart out what she considered to be an ideal schedule, according to what courses she needed to have for college prep, whether she qualified for honors classes, and so forth.

Then a packet was handed out to each student. In it were our grades from the spring semester. In my case, and in Libby's case, our grades were listed, but the packet also had a note saying that

153

our grades were being transferred back to our old schools so they could be a part of our final transfer records. That was fine with me. It didn't change any of my grades. I got all A's, except for phys ed and algebra. I got B's in those courses. I'm not sure what will happen with my algebra grade. At Eagle Point, I was taking a course called Pre-algebra Concepts. The two courses were really different.

Also in the packet were notices about whether we qualified for honors classes. I have been recommended for an honors English class. Jon, of course, has been recommended for Advanced Computing and honors math.

Then, after we filled out our schedules—which took some doing since Libby, Jon, and I tried to see how many classes we could get together—we each went to talk to a teacher who was designated as our "advisor." It was all arranged alphabetically, so Libby, Jon, and I went together under the W's! Our advisor, of all people, was Mr. Grassmyer. He approved our schedules, with the exception that he recommended I take Algebra 1 over since I was missing some of the basics for that course. I'm glad that's what he advised. There were times during the last few weeks when algebra class made about as much sense as mud. Libby is also going to be in Algebra 1.

For the most part, we got the schedules we had decided. Libby wanted to see where her classes were going to be held, so we did a little walk through the halls to find each class. We stopped several times to talk to kids from our previous classes. It's funny how some of the kids are more friendly now that the semester is *over* than they ever were during it. Perhaps they are feeling a little like "new kids" as they face being sophomores. That's an interesting idea to think about.

The three of us had lunch together and after we had cleaned out our lockers—and also cleaned out our gym lockers and turned in our uniforms—we were free to go home. Jon, however, said that he needed to talk to Miss Scaroni about something for a few minutes so I told him I'd wait and walk home with him. There was also something I wanted to do. "I'll meet you at the entrance in a little while," I said. He nodded. "I'll meet you there."

I walked with Libby as far as the main entrance and told her I'd call her tomorrow, probably in the evening after Aunt Beverly and I get back from Benton. (I didn't want to tell her that Jon was going, too. That seemed like telling a secret, somehow.)

And then I immediately walked through the halls out toward the park and then across the park to Emily's Place. I hadn't been there in several days and it felt good to come back. I sat down for a while and thought about all that has happened in the last few weeks since we moved to Collinsville.

I realized that I haven't thought about McKinney College hardly at all in the last two weeks. In fact, I don't think I've thought about it once, except when Aunt Beverly mentioned it as part of her testimony. Somehow I think enduring Collinsville High might not be so difficult after all.

I thought back to what Kiersten had said about being homesick, and realized that I'm not as homesick for Eagle Point as I had thought I would be. I probably should try to talk to Kiersten again about that to see how she's doing. She has seemed a little quiet the last few days.

I also thought about my friends—about how I had met Kimber . . . and then Libby . . . and then Trish. Each friend so different in personality, and yet a friend, nonetheless. I thought about how we had met in such different ways. It's only been a few weeks since I've known them—in Trish's case, less than two weeks!—but somehow, they really seem like *friends*.

I thought about Jon . . .

"I thought I'd find you here." There he was, standing in the archway leading to the courtyard. Jon pretended to knock on an invisible door as he said, "Mind if I come in?"

"Not at all," I said. "Why should I?"

"Well, you sure minded the first time I talked to you here," he said.

"That's because you really startled me," I said.

"Here," Jon said as he pulled a flower from behind his back and held it out toward me.

"Did you pick this from the park?" I asked.

"Yeah," said Jon. "I know that's probably against some rule but I figured it would look better in your hand than it did on that scraggly bush." As Jon reached forward to hand me the flower, he also leaned forward and kissed me on the cheek— very gently, very casually.

I don't mind telling you, Journal, that all of time seemed to come to a stop in that moment. Jon Weaver has not so much as touched me before that—not an arm on my shoulder, or holding my hand, or anything. (You really can't count his helping to pick me up and throw me in the pool at the Wilsons'.) Such a sweet, lovely kiss. It was so quick and so soft I wasn't even sure for a second that it had happened. I took the flower from Jon's hand and I just couldn't look him in the eyes. I'm sure I wouldn't have known what to say.

"Thanks," I said.

"Thank *you*," he said back. Jon sounded very serious. I knew I still couldn't look at him as long as he had that tone of voice. "Thank you for being my friend. I was really dreading the move here to Collinsville, starting a new school and all, but now I think that it just may be one of the best things that has ever happened to me."

"I know what you mean," I said, still staring down toward the base of the fountain.

"I hope—" said Jon.

But before he could get another word out of his mouth, I said—well, actually, I nearly shouted—"That's her!"

"That's who?" said Jon, quickly looking around.

"That's the girl I saw in the Wilsons' yard—the one who came to get her runaway dogs!"

"Where?" said Jon, who by this time had stood up and was looking out the archway into the park. "What are you talking about?"

"There," I said, pointing toward the tintype picture at the base of the fountain, right next to the words "In memory of Emily, 1922–1940."

"You saw *that* girl?" said Jon, with a major tease in his voice. "I don't think so."

"No, it couldn't have been the same girl, silly," I said. "But the girl I saw at the Wilsons' looked just like her! I wonder if Emily was related to her."

"Frankly, Katelyn," said Jon, "I don't remember seeing a girl come into the Wilsons' yard."

"Don't you remember the two white dogs that came running into the yard and the girl in the white dress who came in looking for them?"

"No," said Jon. "Were you seeing ghosts, maybe?"

"No. They were real," I said. "But now my curiosity is really running wild. I'd love to be able to find that girl and talk to her and see if she's related to Emily."

"You've got an entire summer to scout her out," said Jon.

"Yes, and I intend to do so," I said, feeling very determined as I picked up the big sack of stuff from my locker, my purse, and the novel I've been reading—*Christy* by Catherine Marshall—a really good book, by the way.

"You were saying something before I went wild," I said to Jon. "Something along the lines of 'I hope . . .'"

"Yeah," said Jon, with a grin.

"What are you hoping for?" I said.

"Oh, just hoping," said Jon. "I'm just a hopeful guy."

And no matter how much I teased him all the way home, I could *not* get Jon Weaver to tell me what he was hoping for.

One thing for sure, I've got lots of things to hope for, and to think about, and to anticipate this summer . . .

Will the FF Club really take off?

What will happen to Aunt Beverly and Mr. Clark Weaver? Will they ever go out on a date?

Will I get a chance to have a real heart-to-heart talk with Trish?

159

Will Kimber and Dennis get together?

Will I be able to find the girl who looks like Emily?

What will Jon Weaver look like after Aunt Beverly gets finished with his make-over?

The summer is just beginning, and in lots of ways, I feel as if my life in Collinsville has just begun. Still, you know me. I don't like loose ends. So even though I feel full of new beginnings, it's time for this journal to say . . .

The End

—Katelyn Weber
325 Maple Street
Collinsville

An Excerpt from *Friends Make the Difference,*
Book Two in the Forever Friends series:

No sooner had Jon left than the phone rang and
it was Kimber—who had truly exciting news to
share!

"He kissed me," she said quietly, not even both-
ering to tell me who was calling, or to give me
any build-up at all.

"He *did?*" I nearly shouted into the phone.

"Yes!" said Kimber, shouting back into the
phone and laughing at the same time.

"Was it wonderful?" I asked.

"Truly," she said.

"Well, tell me what happened," I said. "All the
details. Start at the beginning."

"There's really not all that much to tell," she
said. "Dennis dropped off you and Jon and then
instead of turning toward my house, he headed for
Libby's house. He dropped her off and when we
got back to my house, I started to get out of the
car, but he held my arm back as I turned to get
out. When I turned around to see what he wanted,
he reached over with his other hand and turned
my head toward him, and then he just leaned over
and kissed me."

"Did he say anything?" I asked. I wished I were
there in person with her. I knew I wasn't doing
the living room sofa any good by jumping up and

down on it—half seated and half on my knees—and crunching up the pillows.

"Not really," Kimber said. "After he kissed me, he just said, 'Good night, Kimber.' And that was all. I got out of the car and went to the house."

"Was it a long kiss?" I asked. "Details, Kimber. I want d-e-e-e-e-tails."

"No. It was just short and nice. I could tell that he kinda wanted to kiss me again, but when he said, 'Good night, Kimber,' I said, 'Good night, Dennis,' and that pretty much broke the spell. He had such a wonderful look in his eyes, though, Katelyn. I thought I was going to melt right then and there."

"Oh, this is so exciting," I said. "Did you tell your mom?"

"I didn't get a chance," said Kimber. "She came around the corner into the hall just as I walked in and closed the door. I guess I must have been leaning back against the door with a dreamy look on my face or something, because she just looked at me and said, 'I hope he wipes the lipstick off his face before he goes into *his* house!'"

Watch for *Friends Make the Difference* at a bookstore near you.